SHANGRI-LA AND OTHER STORIES

Shangri-La and Other Stories

Dani Darius

PARTRIDGE

A Penguin Company

Partridge books may be ordered through booksellers or by contacting:

Partridge India
Penguin Books India Pvt.Ltd
11, Community Centre, Panchsheel Park, New Delhi 110017
India
www.partridgepublishing.com
Phone: 000.800.10062.62

CONTENTS

A PREFACE

A friend once asked me about the kind of stories that I like—where I get my inspiration from; the authors, who move me the most. Yes, there were a few stories that changed the course of my life, the pattern of my thought; authors, who had laid the groundwork.

So, I answered as honestly as I could.

I liked Gauguin's story 'The Wind That Halts.' I very much liked Alexander Vincent Peal's 'The Submerge,' Hirudai Honda's 'The Pink Bird,'; Milton Friedman's 'The Barber's Last Client.'

'Pretty stories they are, friend,' the friend had said.

This quiet acknowledgement of my taste smote me. I fetched a long breath and broke the silence that had been lurking in my heart for so long.

One after another, tumbled down the stories that I took delight in; from behind my ears they unplugged, from the tangle of my hair, from my nostrils; from all the orifices twice over—from my breast pocket, hidden in my socks, pinned to cufflinks, the belt that I was wearing.

Stories like the 'Nakshatras' by Feynman, 'In the Vineyard' by Silverhorn Negroponte, 'A Day in Benares' by Sandracottas, Benjamin Eliot's 'White Seal of Sargasso,' 'Sisyphean's Last Crawl' by Armando Maradona.

Ah, yes, 'Zero-o'-'earo' by Padmapani, which like a Bodhi-tree in one tropic night, was strangled by swiftly enclosing creepers.

Jonny Hay's 'Toupeé Café' was a classic. It wasn't a story. It was civilization steamrolled in a few words.

My friend implied a pause. The day had rolled into the night. The spirit songs were calling.

The stories I've mentioned are but a few in the long list that I so dearly cherish, nay, hold on to my heart like a lost little bird who hasn't yet taken to wings.

It was good that my friend intervened so courteously. As I couldn't have talked forever, I made a pact with myself: to keep silence until I conjure up a slim compilation—wherein the *child* shall speak.

But, what child?

Whose child?

The child in me, or an orphan?

If it is my child, then I'm sorry to say that he really hasn't learned the art of telling a story. *I haven't taught him?* No, I tried my best but his vision fluctuated a lot. He acted mature and sometime, indeed, so full of wisdom and sanity that I was struck. But, then again, his mind rushes hither thither. He goes mad; a compulsive streak he has inherited from me. Perhaps.

There are light strokes of beauty that he catches, yet his temper, his volatility tore apart the light strokes.

Those were the times I used to detest him. Yet, as a father, I have certain responsibilities. We were going separate ways. I felt that keenly: Why! . . . didn't he write on a flyleaf of *Wu-Wei*—that precious volume of aphorisms that never failed to provide a balm to my soul—a mock haiku:

Let me go: Find
A cove
A shade
Me

Let heaven find: You
A cross
A light
Thee

The time I read it, it caused me insufferable anguish and mortification, but I hid my feelings; thought time would allay my fears, but no: This interlarding, in him, of spells of deep quiet broken by a rather feckless violence, continued to grow apace: scrawled all over the wall, scratched on the window, the door, even on my eyeglasses!

I knew it wasn't graphomania, or an afflicted mercury. It was more like veiled shadows of predestination, a breeze teasing a candle flame.

I, however, considered it my sacred duty to collect and collate all his writings and give it to the editor.

This I did, and thus follow the words you're about to read or shred depending on your mood, your propensity or how you view the world.

The child is straying away. He finally did go away. I grieve all the time. He left me no address. No clue, whatsoever, of his whereabouts. 'What shall become of him?' I bemoan.

I went to the police station and filed a missing person report. The police were cordial and they assured me that they were going to find him. It will take time, they said. This country is big. Huge.

Meanwhile, I too shall do my best. I'll go to a shaman if need be. I'll go to a yogi (if there is a breakdown), or to a telepath, an astrologer; a private investigator.

I'll travel till I find my child.

AUTHOR'S NOTE

Though the stories have not been arranged in their order of sequence with any fixed principle as to that of their chronology, I would be remiss not to mention the events and conditions that impelled me to pen them. One way or the other, the context is very Indian for I am an Indian man and my journeys were but peregrinations to those places in northern India, which naturally draw the fancy of young men and women and the old, in the footsteps of former pilgrims. It is like a yokel's awe of things sacred and an escape from the mortality that has ever reminded everywhere. It is not a 'parallel journey'; it is one journey.

Peace here perforce is the pleasure, yet certainly we can—whether formless or wrapped—enjoy more than our resources. Philosophy aside, I, then, the boisterous young man, travelled for pleasure.

Every facet of our lives stands in some relationship to every other, and on the whole, it seems right that an effort should be made to establish such a relationship.

Thus a brief two-day trip to Mcleod Ganj, Dharmashala[1] in the year 2007; the genial hour spent in the company of many good men

---

[1] Dharmashala is the headquarters of Kangra district in the state of Himachal Pradesh, India and is also the seat of the exiled Tibetan government. In Sanskrit, it is a compound word, Dharma-Shala, which, narrowly construed, means a Religious-Abode. In a general sense, the term may be rendered thus: `a temporary resting place or sanctuary for convenience of travelers.' The word currently used for designating the place is Dharamshala—which is non-literary and colloquial. It would be more representative of a highly evolved spiritual-complex resident in that place, if the classical term Dharma—with its wide semantic

and women; the bracing mountain air; the natural exuberance with which I discovered the new and what was alien—on hindsight—fetched me a reflexive tale, 'Shangri-La.'

'Tara' and 'The Mist' on the other hand are chapters from a novel I had a desire to write long back, circa 2000. An undercurrent there was the ongoing breach between the so-called 'state' and the stateless': the deprived tribes of India, blown and buffeted by the neglect of the state for centuries, it has grown into a mount of fire—INSAS rifles, .25 bore guns, SLR and AK-47s; and though there exists this festering wound, though there is spleen, there still remains the Ideal; the aspiration toward the luminous.

A weekend's journey to Rishikesh in 2003, followed by another in a gap of six months and the swiftly changing complexion of the place, inspired me to write a series of interrelated tales, of which there are three in this volume—Bobbing Back, Purple Dhaba and The Fringe: those, which may bear out a semblance of being independent.

There are others, which needed no travelling, like the Colonnade, Perfume, Creatures' All, and The Sentinels. "Needed no travelling" in the sense that I didn't have to catch the midnight bus, or the express train or the tramcar.

Often identities flow into each other in the drag of time, and if in 'Roxanne' there is occupation and defiance, love and karma and where the famous dead become shadows, then 'The Escort' may take us to the junction where we stay or we go.

In publishing this volume of short stories, there were times when I was inclined to give up in despair. It was like trying to write infinite letters in finite envelopes, and when my spirit and health languished, Ms. Leza Lowitz came to my aid and restored my confidence. We never met personally. I was trying my best to be published and I sent a story to her in Japan in 2007, which she liked and encouraged me to

---

connotations—were used in place of Dharam. It is not a hearkening to orthodoxy or the exalted nature of a classical language, but a tribute to the spirit of the place and the people.

keep on writing, urging me to persevere. Like a battering ram, I kept on sending her story after story.

To her, I owe an incalculable debt.

If a collection of stories contain in it a sense and a purpose, then it is my hope that the readers won't see it as a testimony to what I believed at a particular time or an autobiographical document, but a cry emerging from the outpost of reason.

Dani Darius
6 July 2010
Haridwar, India

SHANGRI-LA

Hey man, sometimes you get ensconced in the rotten womb of time, but the rotten womb of time is a whore's and you can't get over the defilement. This is what afflicted my friend D.

I got a mail from him from the psychiatric ward of the institute of mental sciences in Delhi; a quirky archaic mail that put me off. The language, I mean (among other things). He was quite okay when we traveled together to that schizoid hill station called McLeod Ganj, which, he said was the place from where his mother came. It's the seat of morons and grasshoppers—Divine kin of the primitive order of fogies. D thinks otherwise. You understand!

For your introduction, D's half-Tibetan; the other half, Indian. He insists on calling the river Jumna—'Tsang-po.' Imagine that! I call it the sewer canal.

A few days after our trip, he slid down the pole of sense and had to be admitted to the wards. I had seen him talking to himself as if he were someone else. He even wrote letters to himself and replied to them, but I never thought it was symptomatic of a deeper illness.

Anyway, I share with you this letter, or rather, fragments of it, as certain portions could only be read by the 'noble' savage. Then I shall put forth my wisecracks on reality and try hard not to be smutty.

> Hi Dani,
>
> It is with a heavy heart that I have to write this down, my friend. I don't want to drag you into my dark thoughts again. But there are things that I have to tell you. At times little things loom large. And you've known about all my strange yearnings and despondency for so long now that I take it for granted that you'll understand. You remember the

1

brass deity I got from McLeod Ganj? Yes, the same deity, our 'Beggar King': He—of long fingers and noble limbs, sitting like a child with that brooding heavy-lidded 'beyond hope' expression on his face. You perhaps didn't observe what he was clutching: a mascot resembling an emaciated owl (my mother thought it was a mongoose) in his right fist and a rolled up parchment in his left. So many *kalpas* have flown and he might have been a world conqueror at any end of time.

Since that day, I have been trying to discover his identity, albeit with inconstant interest. I had surveyed the whole pantheon of Tibetan deities, without any success.

My father reckoned he was the 'Mahakal' of a Katmandu temple, the sentinel of karmic time. That would have been interesting, even plausible, incredibly tired as he appeared to me, but I never deferred to this conjecture.

He seemed less obscure than the series of obscure images I had seen in a rudimentary sanctum in the temple complex of Konark: that of Saturn and Jupiter, of Rahu and Ketu and the two other portentous gods whom I cannot recall now. Therefore, I guessed, that our deity wasn't as ominous as I have come to believe him to be. But one cannot say about such things.

Last night, I finally brought myself to remove him from my bed where he was lying idle among the books. Curious spell he had cast over me, much like the Tibetan Book of the Dead once did: that evil book (I call it the Book of Dead Tibetans) that by some strange association, I had come to see as an emblem of my misfortunes. I won't invoke it anymore. I have spoken to you about it, didn't I?

Well, perhaps our 'deity' may be one of the Bodhisattvas.' I had often thought of that weird and wonderful idea. After all, why would he still be wearing a crown on his wilting head? Crowned by the numberless lost souls he had saved from perdition!

However, he certainly does not possess the youthful and sensual mien of the potential Buddha's. I am perhaps wrong about the sensuality part. You would agree that he is sensual in a serene but somber manner. Doubtless, he was once possessed of capricious humors and a fiery rage. But he had become quieter over time. Passions cooling off . . . Silently reflecting on the ever-growing pile of suffering that was his. Not dead, yet not quite alive; hovering in the hazel zone. Possibly, though, He had become senile—a man, well past his prime, dreaming of past dreams, heavy and laden and moth-colored . . . Clutching on to the bird of darkness and vision and the 'Word.'

. . . How wonderfully you strum the guitar, my friend! You catch onto tunes and remember for me the lyrics of never-heard-of songs. If it weren't for your sweetness, I would have never come across the deity. But then, all you had in mind when we rode back was the monkish chants of the hymn. That was a funny refrain and a little melancholy too! You had said that it had a strange entrancing effect and I had agreed. It wasn't a hymn either. Rather, now I feel, it was a song of love mellowed down by exile and the faintly burning youth. I'm sure you still have the tune on you but I've lost it. So, when I say it was a love song, then I am only trying to construct the fire by meditating on the embers. Even as my eyes fetch me memories, my ears ain't so keen. I suppose I envy you for that. If you cannot remember the sounds, then all your traveling is in vain. It might well have been another excursion around our glitzy township. Glitzy and inane, hey!

So it might have been and so it has been, now that I try to recall the sound of the restaurant. Or was it a hotel?

. . . Ya, hotel Shangri-La. That's where we had heard the tune; when we ate more than our appetite could summon. The few exotic dishes, whose names sounded like incantations; but we weren't so venturesome, Dani, and we settled for the mundane fare. The bland and the grand momo's—fried, baked, boiled—morning, noon and evening; chop suey and special tofu noodles; chocolate custards and the chocolate pancake, we never managed to finish. Toast with strawberry jam, butter and honey for breakfast, and those heart-shaped poached eggs, oh! And our funny little tune played out on the Chinese disc-player by our somnolent lama.

He was heartbroken for sure, playing up the jig again and again to alleviate some distant pain. Could we ever be so lavish with our tips, hiding them under the menu card for our little waiter? But the monk could still see us clearly from behind the counter, where all the while he was adding up the prices in that medieval calculator. Did our little fella' share his tip with *her*, I wonder!

. . . How we had wished that our delightful little supper would go on forever. It came to us like manna . . . Isn't it strange that we entered it just as we were caught in the sudden squall . . . Exactly how we had discovered Tushita . . . And we saw the same equanimous nun in her maroon habit, levitating with her heaving umbrella and managing a perfect *tour en l'air*. Just serendipity or were the gods the usher, directing us to a secret address?

. . . Tushita . . . No, I'm wrong. That couldn't have been the name of the bookshop. The bookshop had nothing to do with the heavens. But then, I never found so many books in one place, at one time. So many, that I was *looking* for. There was the Milindapanha, Kawabata and Saint-Hilaire. There were Hesse and Ramses and the Sutras of Nagarjuna.

Those delightful bookmarks, which I still have, seven of them, carrying little charming pictures, quaint messages or a futile appeal on the obverse. Little Lhasa, Tibet World, Thank You India, etc. 'An appeal to the youth of the free world' to shun Beijing 2008 . . . With the rebel bookkeeper (our glint-eyed Ho Chi Minh) thanking us over and over again. He needn't have worried.

We'll never make it to the Olympics, anyhow. There are mountains between us. Between youth and glory. Between glory and oblivion. Imagine, you and I going over the roof across the debris of lamaseries, trekking over the Himalayan snow to participate in the triple jump!

I'll tell you a little secret. He made it, our Ho, and returned disillusioned when his deity called upon him to renounce the guns. For piety. For peace. The resistance had turned inward, since. That was 1974 before we were born— and that wasn't the last time he felt betrayed. His only dream now is to go there and die. He has transferred his accounts to his wife's name and has all but wound up his affairs. But surely, that shall not end his bitter tryst with exile . . . .

The deity is like the mountain. *His* deity. They say he is the compassionate Buddha incarnate—the living Avalokiteshvara. Shining radiant above the mist; sometimes claimed by the clouds and obfuscated; moldy, crumbling pigments of ancient paintings like Ajanta . . . And, the termites are crawling uphill slowly. Soon they'll gobble up. The disheveled Frenchman was right, 'Noisee . . . too noisee . . . Stupiditee. . . . I shall never again return; It wasn't like this eight years back.' Oui, we weren't there eight years back. Too busy making careers. Oui, absolut madness . . . *Au revoir Ami*! That's it . . .

How much more could the slender streets hold? You can't keep a habitat floating when the gravity sucks at it, claws it down to the commons. You were right, Frenchman! The crazy tuft of silver hair, flying over your skull like a frayed prayer-pennant wasn't out of place. Rain-washed, sun-bleached, withering mountains peopled by a lost civilization: a motley procession of cast-out pilgrims sticking together. The same souvenirs sold in shop after shop and the proprietary colors changing ever so softly: the language becoming more comprehensible, more familiar. That's fine. That's happening elsewhere too. Not so starkly perhaps.

An image oftentimes begins to dance in my eyes. Last year, when I happened to travel to Manali (which—as we know—has a residual Tibetan community, unlike this place), I saw a drunken Tibetan woman with a cigarette between her lips, gyrating slowly in front of the Krishna temple in the main square of the Manali mall, with her breasts half exposed and hordes of tourists gawking at her. She was crazy, and the authorities left her to herself. Very generous of them, I suppose. If you ever happen to travel to Manali, don't forget to give her a quarter of whiskey. I was too stingy. Too tight, man!

Shangri La! I still remember the high colors on her cheeks, yet I have forgotten the chime of her voice.

Perhaps, you might remember still. In her aromatic confine, she could transmute as if by magic, the ordinary into the delectable. She returned my smile so many times and her gaze was so frank, that I cast my eyes low. That was the last day of our stay. Wasn't she anxious and embarrassed when she cooked the wrong noodle dish? The little boy was apologizing for her. I could hear her speak through him. She needn't have bothered. We would have devoured everything served on the platter; so hungry were we . . . .

15 October 2007

The letter was super-scribed as 'urgent.'

It took a while for me to sense what was so very urgent about it. I would like to jot down a few pertinent points regarding this so-called 'urgent' letter and why I consider it a perversion of the facts. Truth must be told.

☙ ✻ ❧

There is no such restaurant as Shangri-La. It is D's invention. Yes, we did go to an eatery during our stay in McLeod Ganj; it was located in a dark alley to the Southeast of the monastery. If I remember correctly, its name was Tushita—a nondescript ramshackle place and Oh, such a sanctimonious name! Furthermore, it wasn't an establishment run by the lamasery, as he seems to indicate. I saw no girl with ruddy cheeks cooking the food (with whom he seems to have struck up some sort of personal concord). I know that a little boy waited on us, but we never gave him a tip that was more than our meager pockets could allow.

We once did muffle a laugh when we saw a swirling nun, tossing in the rain with her cavernous umbrella. But the comic apparition didn't come to tickle us for a second time. The color maroon was everywhere . . .

There were several bookshops in the two square kilometers radius, which constitutes the heart of the place. D bought several second-hand books during our three-day stay, including those he mentions. But he got them from not one, but several different shops.

There was nothing remarkable about the shopkeepers. If he thinks that the old man, from whose shop he got two or three tattered old editions, was a former rebel then he's just being fanciful, as is his wont. It satisfies his romantic imagination, nothing more.

It is true, that a CIA-backed resistance force operated from Nepal in the early seventies, running raids against Chinese military outposts in the Tibetan plateau, and the members of that ragtag group gave up their arms at the behest of the Dalai Lama in 1974; but D gratuitously drags our old man into the fracas and dresses him up in guerrilla attire!

My poor friend talks about the drunken Tibetan woman in Manali square. Well, there may have been several drunken women in Manali: Tibetan, locals and ageing hippies who lost their heads binging on alcohol and ganja, reminiscing about the decades of pot-power; the many who got stuck in time. Contrariwise, she may just be another figment of his creepy imagination.

The disheveled Frenchman, whom we did meet, could perhaps be counted among those who were vainly trying to resurrect the past, searching for missing mates and beguiling places in the once-liberated zone of their younger days. Alas, he's just another lost soul like my friend.

It didn't really take me by surprise when D suddenly began to empathize with the exiled Tibetans in McLeod Ganj. I now remember how it all began. An old Tibetan oracle, whose special province is the interpretation of past lives, told him that he was a snow leopard in his previous birth. When I first heard this absurd theory, I found it so nonsensical that I split my sides laughing. But impressionable as my friend is, it caught his fancy. Thus, while in McLeod Ganj, he whined that the whole place should be demarcated as Tibet and there should be some sort of control over the spaces that lead up to the hill. This, he said, would preserve a semblance of the culture and its manifestations, that are slowly being eroded and becoming unidentifiable with the local ones. It is obvious that such a thing is happening, yet it is unconscionable that a place be preserved for its culture and maintained as such through time. Will it do any good if a living, throbbing mountain retreat were treated as a reserve sanctuary for the near extinct . . . ? Hasn't the government already done enough?

Even when I read the letter, I balked at the word 'termite,' D's pejorative for the locals of that place. Hasn't he got some Indian blood in him? You don't spit on yourself, do you, D? Yet, when I think about it, I've got some Tibet in me too. Nevertheless . . .

I cannot understand why he dwells so much on the deity. For all I know, D is a non-believer, or at least he projected himself as such, and was never given to superstition.

I couldn't see anything on the deity that even vaguely resembled a totem owl (or a mongoose). On the other hand, I believe, I saw that he was holding onto a scabbard: the dagger in it might have fallen off a long time ago. Then again, what profane rapture an innocuous brass-cast statue can hold is completely beyond my comprehension. It maybe, that D had come to identify the stupor and the sickness that had alighted in his soul with that of the idol.

My friend was much moved by my guitar playing, and why shouldn't he have been? He doesn't possess any musical sense whatsoever. Even if I had struck the wrong chords, he wouldn't have known. The tune he talks about so emotively is neither a psalm nor a plaintive love song. It is just a simple highland Tibetan folk-ballad interspersed with a liberal use of gongs and cymbals and hollow pipes. Its dreary, dithyrambic beat renders it an outlandish preternatural quality, which inveigles the uninitiated, not us!

It is pertinent to mention here that I am a failed guitarist and that's perhaps why we became friends in the first place. He's a little lost. Indeed, there is an inert ripple of sorrow in him; as if a single little heave had frozen in the remote backwaters of an unknown sea. I'm fagged out too. Seditious whispers roll in the sand and one day the *khampa* in me shall ride off on a white stallion. In the serpentine walks of McLeod Ganj—across half-mile slices of crumbling time—I seek myself, my address.

Therefore, I confess, that I too am not beyond impressions and get carried away by new and novel sensations. Thus, when we were traveling back, I did have the primitive music on my mind. I heard it fleetingly when it came billowing out from the shady alley where our restaurant was located.

Before we boarded the bus on the 6th of July, we had a light meal there. It was then that I saw her. Oh . . . What a rosy tart!

D thought she was the cook, as the air around her was smoky and redolent of lemongrass and the fiery Szechuan. Maybe she had managed a hearth before, but judging from her darting gamin-like eyes and the waft of two-penny perfume, I inferred that she was one of the saucy wenches who used to go there to get cheap grub (and to hunt for clients?).

. . . And I thought she smiled at me, not him.

And what a maniacal smile it was!

———— ◆ ————

COLONNADE

Every day, these days, I dream early in the morning that I'm crossing the Strand road to the old mint of Calcutta, where James Princep—who had once deciphered the Brahmi script of Asokan times—was the assay master.

I walk across the mint colonnaded in Greco-Roman style and cross that refinery to another sumptuous sanctum—a huge dream, etched in marble.

For three days, I dreamed the same dream before a sad little twerp begged me to buy his roasted chickpeas.

I did buy fifty grams of that trash, not so much out of guilty slummer feelings perhaps; but more out of a visceral desire to shake off the dream of magnanimous proportions. The marble atriums still hung-over and thence I wondered!

As I was trained in Hindustani, I asked him whether he had anything to eat. He said he did indeed, but not chickpeas.

His audacity curdled the butter sour and I muttered under my breath: 'You bloody . . . Of low cunning.'

I opened my Tiffin box and offered him butter-laced bread that Mary had packed the very morning with such finesse and dollops of love. The toast was perfect.

He took a bite and perhaps did not delight in it so much as Mary would have appreciated, for the very next moment there was a yellow splash on my white *opus classicum*. He seemed to go into a writhe-fit attack. I clenched my hanky in his mouth lest he bit his tongue; and then, he winked at me. I could not help a slow gurgle of laughter and asked him his name.

Now it's literary to say that he's got the same name as mine; and therefore, I wonder, whether he was a sleuth, a fan, a *jalebi* winding around me in ghee—that refined butter that Gentoo's make of cow-milk to worship the flavor of their peculiar pantheon of gods . . . And time.

PURPLE DHABA

It was quite green last year: lemon green walls, and this year it was lilac. Purple Dhaba. The proprietor was a handsome man—very much the same as the signboard. Now if you ever cross the Laxmanjhula bridge over to the right bank; turn right, and make your way through the narrow streets lined with shops—you don't have to go too far before the handsome sign catches your attention. And, if you want to feel at home in the Dhaba—as road-side restaurants are often called—let you be aware, that there is no such thing as a home that you'd find there. The ground floor's rectangular face was presumably for Indians and the first floor more to foreign tastes—overlooking the Ganges and other lofty scenarios.

An attempt was made to perk up the first floor in the style of the Middle East (which constituted of Israeli youths mostly) with Persian rugs, long pillows and smoke pipes, but as you can see, the proprietor could not bring himself to change the essential character—and upon second thoughts—out of place, if he did. The long pillows were now a comfortable nest for the rats, the rug had starry holes in it, and the smoke pipe could be transmuted to suit the piper of Hamlyn.

Therein, where you find yourself at home.

☙ ✺ ❧

It was at the *Indian* floor facing the street, that the Japanese middle-aged man, sipping on the lemon-mint tea became edgy, and in spite of himself had to ask the smart lady—whose back he faced—where she hailed from, in his off-broken English (but we wish not to make fun of accents and races, so we create a semblance of a proper dialogue).

'Oh, you're talking to me,' the woman half-turned to look over her shoulders. 'I'm now . . . err . . . in Toronto.'

'Often you come to India.'
'Well all South-East Asia really.'

She was presumably displeased by the interjection in her reveries. It would seem so, since she screwed up her eyes and made a face, puckered her lips, which was testament of the many struggles she had to put up with; god knows what?

'You like this place,' continued the Japanese man.
    'Yea,' she replied, without turning back.

'Why?'
    'For the same reasons.'

'Where else have you been to?'
    'A lot of places.'

'You've been to Calcutta.'
    'Well yes, to the Nirmal Hriday.'
'Oh, my niece too had been there. Mother Teresa and she's still working as a . . . as a . . .
. . . Volunteer,' she volunteered to get him the right word.
'Yes, yes . . . Thanks—'

She turned around and stoked up a smile. A very recognizable smile it would seem.
    'Indeed,' she whiffed; her blue gaze resting upon the twinkling, shifting, restless' eyes of the stocky middle-aged man with bags under his eyes and just for a second, his youthful, nervy voice struck her as different

'. . . Ummmm my sister worked there. In fact many years . . .'
'Oh, then she must know Yumi.'
    'She joined the UNHCR five years back. Was your niece there, then?'
'No madam.'

She turned around and gazed at the streets and the handsome profile of the Punjabi proprietor, ever-the-same every year. She would seem tired, that half her orange juice she barely sipped.

'. . . You come here for yoga madam.'
    'Not quite.'

'A lot of people come here around for yoga. It amazes me that Japanese girls come too!'
    'What's there to be amazed about? For Reiki they come too.'
'Ahhhh, its news to me. I can't believe.'

Then after a small pause he asked 'Do you also—'
    'Sometimes.' Her voice a whimper.

'You mean you come here often.'
    'As suits . . .

'Oshhhh . . . You must be joking ma'am. You stay in India.'
    'I can stay anywhere I like in.'

'Why so ma'am?'
    'I've got an English language teaching license . . . that's universally applicable.'
    'O-ho . . . oh . . . I see I see . . .'

'. . . *Wha'dya'see old man?*' She thought, and smirked inwardly and with a rather brutal twist, she swivelled her plastic chair and gazed straight at the Japanese man and with a wry, wispy tone hissed: You come here for yoga, mista?'
    'Oh no no, no . . . I don't need to.'
'Pourquoi . . . Why so?' and for the first time she crumpled her face in vexation.

And the Japanese man should be very afraid. And afraid he was.

'I'm gymnast mademoiselle.'
    'Tsk . . . Gymnastics is not the same as yoga.'

'Well,' he sighed and his eyes were laughing sadly and yet it was contagious in a drifting way. Dithering, he said raspy: 'I was in Melbourne . . .

'What's that gotta' do . . . !'

'Melbourne 76' . . . got a silver on the pommel horse.'

PERFUME

I see two streams of smoke rising from the cigarette tracing two identical patterns in space. They fork up, hang lazy—then diffuse in a tangled mass somewhere. There is no sweet chemistry to coax my senses, no enticement to believe, to recollect; I simply watch the smoke. While rising at an angle, they maintain perfect symmetry: forming quick and even loops at an increasing distance to each other. The loops themselves form an interesting crescendo of images. At times, they appear like the flared capitals of a Corinthian pillar, then they seem like the cochlea of a snail and dangle in space in their respective coordinates for a dithering while. Yet again, they simply eddy, turn slowly or are just plain sticky.

If you look keenly, you'll observe the edges blur away; but for each curl, and indeed, at every point on their languid course, is an inner fiber of strong whitish-blue, that is loath to disintegrate. I wonder why I can see it so clearly tonight!

I see the crust of ashes at the burning end of the stub and I'm amazed by the color of the fire. It quickens my flesh and gives the night an enchanted feel. I'm so deeply moved by the fiery orange of the smoldering eye: as if the fire is of timeless nostalgia like the disk of a tiny sun.

When you hold a candle in a dark room and watch its reflection on your eyes with a looking glass, the irises seem to flicker and you get a glimpse deep within yourself and so you fancy, but I never imagined that a cigarette can hold such mortal rapture.

Now, like unfurling ribbons, the milky patterns gush toward me but stream left to the broken glass and I realize that the tramcar T3-R is moving again. There is an aisle between the rows of empty seats and I had noticed, in spite of my meditations, the only other passenger—a woman—getting off.

The 'No smoking' message glares down at me and there's a skull up there too! Three faded pamphlets, bearing the emblem of the hammer and the sickle, dangle half-torn and tattered, above the window to my right and flutter in the bracing wind picked up by the moving vehicle.

I had let the cigarette burn all the way down after the last puff that I had dragged two minutes ago. Now, I flick off the burrowing end and see a tiny speck of fire, tracing a short arc, as it hits the patchy cobblestone overlaid with fresh tarmac and bounces off beyond my field of vision.

I crane my neck to catch a glimpse of the receding image of the woman. Her braids sway ever so slightly in the chiaroscuro glow of the streetlights and there is a darkness out there, waiting to consume her too.

I find a fifty Euro note in her purse; a half-used dove-pink max-factor lipstick, a small cosmetic cabinet, a lubricant with local anesthetic properties.

. . . A passport size photograph of a little blue-eyed child with a pale face and a lost expression; a silk handkerchief, redolent of a perfume whose fragrance I thought I had forgotten.

She turned fleet footed at the corner of the street, crossed the marble statue of St. Veronica; slowed her pace when the blue luminous serpents, coiling in a death grip, the massive torso of Lacoön and his sons, spouted pale-green water.

The moon could be seen as a golden quavering blotch in the little pool from where the entwined man rose. For a ponderous while, she stood there vacuously watching the image of a mythic struggle. Then she brushed with a tissue the few drops of water that had whizzed down with a truant current of air and had spurted the military-green leather outfit above the frosted-metal buckles.

A wizened old accordionist and a godlike Negro youth with a mandolin were serenading under the dream-gaze of Veronica and while the old musicians creased face assumed a hint of irony when he noticed the *drifting* woman; she sighed furtively, when she observed, despite herself, the Negro address the *sculpted* woman alone, as if he too was on his way to the Calvary and *she* would come down from her lonely perch to wipe with her head cloth, his beautiful dark face.

There was a time when she used to wear her hair in an elegant coiffure; now she tied her braids into a bun and heard the limpid notes of a sad-sweet madrigal waft across the little plaza. And now, they stopped playing, for a little drizzle had begun to trail on them.

She hastened her steps, and took refuge under the stretched tarpaulin of a renovaré roadside café and sat over the wreckage of a bronze bust of the 'Dictator,' lying face down and riveted to the concrete to form an impressive Art-Nouveau set. There were other such busts—topsy and turvy, innovatively transformed by the proprietor for a solid kind of cushion for the new age customers.

She thought of little Anatolé who must be having his meal at this hour in the orphanage of Nevitskja, five streets and ten miles away near the wharf of the Black Sea.

She had come fifty minutes too early to her assignation time with Vlado—the Brute' as he'll come down from the commissaire's office and wait for her call for there to pick her up on his way. His number was on a slip of paper in a secret fold of her purse and just to make sure, she reached for it on an inside flap of her jacket. It wasn't there.

Two stations away was the tram terminal and she retraced her steps and scurried across the plaza to hire a homing cab. There were still a good forty-five minutes on her.

❦

The conductor was locking up the cabin when she came and anxiously she requested him to open up the back compartment. He complied obligingly. She was lucky she could find her way through the junk of scrap lines and the maze of rusty, decommissioned trams.

The faint smell of marijuana—along with ylang-ylang and heady Russian leather hung in a yellow haze and she winced inexplicably. She could now see her purse at the exact location where she had expected it to be. She peeped inside and saw the fifty Euro note, her cosmetic chamber, the lipstick and the lubricant; the phone number of the brute. That's all she could glean.

She couldn't find the photograph of the child. Nor could she find the lavender silk kerchief, which she had dabbed liberally with the remains of a perfume, that a solitary man crossing the last of the lines at the end of the terminal, sniffed with a catch in his throat—every now and often.

BOBBING BACK-RISHIKESH

White puffed-up belly, spread eagled, bobbing rhythmically in the green swirl of the Ganges just under my gaze, first thing, as the hoar mist cleared with the early shaft of light. Tattered plastic bags thrown up by the river clung on to the hind legs. Solemn chants to Savitri—the long-lost deity—floated in, like time wasn't there. I lit up another cigarette.

On the plastic wash line a bra hung limply—cup C, reminded me of mother. O Mother, its good you were there in the city. The city has no religion, no waft of camphor and ghee from sacrificial fires to supplicate the gods, no effort to freeze nostalgia, no irrational yearning for melancholy.

Later in the day, an old German eccentric introduced himself to me. 'Your deutsch ist bedder dzan myne anglish . . . Donz you ever go Germany?'
. . . But Herr . . . Goethe and Schopenhauer, Shlegel and Hesse . . . Alex Michaels—
'No nein,' he got angry. 'I'm from der not syne. Here de people are zimple und varm. Dere they don care for old volks.'
He even gave me his card and told me that for six months, he will stay here by the holy waters and then he'll move. He was enamored with old Delhi: the vibrant colors, the character. I had seen no vibrant colors so I smiled. He was an East German who had immigrated to Frankfurt. I could vaguely understand.
He offered me a cigarette, 'Benson and Hedges!' I said, 'Ich raucht nicht in India auf front of elders,'—Then I took one. He held up his lighter for me and said, 'Danke Schoen.'

Germany—didn't I once enroll in Max Muller Bhavan? How much had I wanted to study philosophy? What rapture was there in its music, science . . . Football?

❧

The bloated corpse of the macaque was heaving up and down—down the flight of stairs, in the simmering haze of the mid-afternoon sun; the blinding rapier of the beggar's aluminum bowl—pulsating; the glint in the Sadhu's eyes when his 'Hari Om' took on a deeper intonation, as he saw me walking down the bend with a hat on.

Brother *Sadhu*, I know you; I am acting too. A week of bathing in the Ganges for an hour from 11 to 12, not using a sunscreen or a fairness lotion is bringing about my true colors. In a day or two I'll be nutty brown—no hat—I'll have to go back Baba—back to work—back to my brethren in Delhi . . . Mother-fuckers and sister-fuckers . . . Crass music and TV breaking news on cricket, dirty political shibboleth or Bollywood . . . Thanklessness and divide. One chink in the armor and a thousand arrows would come rushing in.

Oh Baba, the waters has been good; just across, on the other bank, in an isolated spot—foreigners were bathing—bikinis or nude; yet unbeknown to them, it was a burning *ghat*, where once upon a time necromancers had a field day and young widows willingly threw themselves upon the crackling pyres.

❧

I had snapped my sacred thread long back—my emblem of Brahminhood. I prefer to excite refined people's attention by saying that I'm somewhere between Communism and Buddhism. O yeah!

I shaved my head and phrenologically speaking, I appear just like a *shramana*; that is when I'm bareheaded! When I walk, I cast my eyes low, try to keep a noble countenance (with the help of diazepam of course). Folks are impressed. I've got a cultivated gait—my military-green hat, the slant perfect—is still on. Foreigners would admire, the locals would be confused; the discerning may think I am from the Garhwali Regiment, a lonesome soldier on a vacation.

Last night a yoga guru tried to touch me; he said he saw his father. *He said, in me, he saw his father.* I shrugged off and went outside. There was chill—there was the mind-numbing gurgle of the river— there was the silver bridge swaying madly in the high wind coming down the steep crevice of the hills flanking the river.

There was the bobbing bus and the asymptote.

———•———

PUFFED RICE WITH RAISINS

My father served me puffed rice with raisins. Late afternoon. Father's unique improvisation.

All days go to return bright and blessed—the more I look into his deep eyes: Me and my soul.

I turn the photo album.

I had repeatedly checked the inroads he had made into me.

I, the austere agnostic; he, the erratic devout. He's the cataract jumping off the rocks—moulding, shaping, grounding the years; I, the silence of the pools before the leap. He's the bronze-skinned that exudes perfume; I, the poisonous shrub!

He—the olive tree that distills a tear, the scented Calamus. I—a sickly colored nard leaf, inclining to whiteness.

He taught me a backhanded scoop of the hockey stick that could've been a world-turner . . . yes . . . I only used it to break the nose of the opponents.

I count the number of raisins, also the number of rice. It is puffed not boiled, thus easier to count. I shall go again to the river to listen to the sounds. He takes to the sea.

I'm Solon to his Croesus.

He's cheery, placid, childlike, serene in his brilliance. His god— the all-generous God. I'm the solemn, the rebel, fuming at the gods: '*dues ultor*'—that vindictive emanation of human imagination . . .

O man, I'm confused today. He just served me puffed rice and I'm bloody thinking of great things. *Must I not make the tea?*

As child, he had much to say to me—Kissinger's voice, his diction, his wit; about Oppenheimer's interpretation of The Gita: *If the effulgence of a thousand suns were of a sudden to blaze forth; The sky, even that would not resemble the majesty of that exalted being . . . ,* That I am . . . *I become death.'* His Sanskrit pronunciation so perfect—the syllable, the word, the captivating tenor.

Also, about Liza Meitner, Annapurna Devi; of Jibonananda Das, Sombhu Mitra, Nazrul Islam . . . Tagore . . . Shakespeare, Ramakrishna, Fidel, Che, Lumumba . . . Kennedy . . .
A real complex pantheon.

I thought of the Buddha and Alexander.

Each page of the Bhagvad Gita—that divine song, I embossed with semen.
He had not the wish to go beyond the Galilean transform, though he was better at mathematics than me; I went past the Lorenz but in deference to his emotions, I stalled my progress; my intellect.
I was explaining to him *zeit und sein* (or was it *sein und zeit*) while he was supping that day, a fish-bone got stuck in his palate and the consequent blob of rice to down it with no effect, and the sputtering, hawking cough—that little retch, or Hepar Sulphur, for he was the homeopath.
There was one thing that held us together all our lives. He was his mother's child, he confessed. He lost his world at twelve when his mother passed away after her eighth infant. He said he suckled on his mother until the ripe age of eleven (he wasn't kidding); I was my mother's child—and mother is always, ever. He joked her nipples were too big for my lips.

The puffed rice: 400338. The raisins: 1100 at the last count.

Mother, *Mother*, brown fog of a winter night, gets my mind a salver curiously inlaid—ten and fifty furlongs, I'll draw you to the assembly of worshippers before the temple of the goddess Hera.
Father needed no pandering to foreign gods. He was happy with his Jagannath—that primal god of the tribal's.
Am I going too high, too deep? Forgive me. That's propensity, ambition, genetics; wrath.
This silent hour, this golden grief . . .

Father! Could you tell them who I am?
Could you tell them who am I . . . Father . . .

I turn a page of the moth-eaten photo album with black corner-tabs peeling off.

There is mother.

O ROXANNE

Behind every man there's a wall. Behind me, there is a shadow. The whites of my eyes reflect the mad swirl of the Hydaspes. Sprays of blood speckle the dwindle of my black coat. When I crossed the river, the monsoon night, the drawl of time touched me. I gazed at myself. The man astride: a sweet tremble; a sunray.

The Mirs of Badakshan to this day pride that their horses are my descendants. Fair glory in the darkening mist. Centaurs lost between the prophet and his majesty 'Ishkander': the two horned.

Time is a rubbish bin. Entropy is actual. The mock of tears a genome—the face of the Bamian was yours, O Sogdian princess.

Hey you . . . kind of like to inform you of hearsay. When time had come for mama, she perched on the birth stool and went into labor. Mama's boyfriend, the Dionysian lover of Pharaonic origin, urged her: No hurry . . . contain yourself. Struggle against the pressure of nature. Reel off the pain . . . Darling . . . look at that. Zeus is clutching the serpent. Nah . . . Now I see your beautiful breasts . . . beautiful, *beautiful.* Scorpios nigh the horizon. The sun's bright. He doesn't like the beasts of heaven yoked together and going backward—will kick him who's born this hour, hell out of heaven.

Grip yourself strong girl. Cancer dominates the Cardo and Saturn, as you know, was a victim of a prank by his children. They castrated him at the roots spriggy bush and hurled him into Neptune of the seas. Now, dead god Pluto maketh way to the majestic Jupiter. Hold tight, for if you give birth now . . . you get a eunuch.

Hold your breath, think of Hades. The poxed-moon in her bull-drawn chariot has dropped off the zenith to descend once again to temptation and is now embracing the olive-skinned herdsman Endymion. He gets to die of fire.

There he passeth—Mercury. *Remind* of Diogenes, the open-masturbating odd ball; of Pindar, so long dead. The emerald-horned, next to the ill-omened star. Pindar shall wait in the noble ashes of Thebes . . . and you'll give birth to a quarrelsome pedant, a monster.

Ufff . . . Jupiter again! Deflowerer of virgins, sprung of the loins of Europa, is now high in the murky rivulet between Aquarius and the fish. Just a moment milady . . . will be a laughing stock. Not so the archer, but the bow is broken. Patient, love. The arrow should strike the sky.

Mars—lion-headed lover of mules and peace, but the sun again reveals him naked and armed in the adulterous bed—shall only raise a great commotion around himself.

Ah, there she comes—bed-loving Venus—mother of Cupid, the killer of swine-headed Adonis. Capricorn is high, Libra is in the ascendant. I can see the moon wax dapple in a blur mist. Whoever is born in this chair of benefaction will take on the luster of the women of Byblos in a man's body. Slow, slow turn the horned Ammon—shall be designated as world ruler. OPEN UP NOW.

. . . *To die the gall of his birth star . . . thirty-two years eight months.*

. . . And I straight fell to the ground . . . there wasn't even a cushion . . . and the tottering palace of Pella was shaken.

When my cuckolded pa, Philip the conqueror, saw mom, he said: 'Let him be raised in the memory of my son by my previous wife, who died.'

To make a long story short, I was weaned by a nursemaid, while mama spurted her milk in naked orgy by the wild flames of serpentine groves. And, the king of Macedon was confused. Alpha-male that he was, so confused, he began to be called Konfukhos. He thought that I no way resembled him. My hair, a bonfire—neither styling-grease nor pomatum had the slightest effect on it. My eyes, asymmetrical, the left one higher than the right; my teeth exuded a black light.

Now did he sire me or was I an apparition, drifting rather like a dream through the city invoked by mama? Her oral assurance that I was of the line of Zeus.

Thus, my conception . . .

How remote is our destiny, princess; now, that you're in a musk deer. The night he cavorted in his chamber sozzled, with his Persian muse and the soft wistful Hephaestion, I heard the rustle of your silk robe. Diaphanous! Blue spars of clouds played on the amber moon and from my stone-bound stable, I pawed the ground and snorted; then neighed discreet. You had looked toward me but all you could've seen was the white-blaze, a horned-triangle emblazoned on my forehead—the legend, the martyr: the ox-brand. From the darkness, I was gazing at you.

You're not a stag and I no more the perception of Xenophon; no more the wings of Pegasus. My each stamp a cymbal, deep furrowed hooves, so broad were my chest, my neck an arch like Homer's gamecock, my mane unruly, clotted; and I was higher than any horse shall ever be; my legs a rippling dance of muscle, my padded back, my deep haunches. Your Thessalian battle-charger.

You are the spirit of a Moschus now . . . And I. What am I? They call him here, Kastouri. This land, a no-man's land—Kashmir. Seek the deep glens, the higher ledges, for huntsmen lust after you. They would tie up the blood collected at *his* navel; cut it away. The navel is the chord they seek. You might have not seen it. Do you know it's about the size of a dove's egg and contains a clotted, oily, friable matter, darkish brown in color—the essence.

The Sun was up: **MAY 326**, the slaughter complete. I reared up and neighed a rattle scream, and turned on my hind legs only to glare at my shadow, one more time, right in front of me, mimicking every flicker of my ache. The little vessel who carried the glory of a celestial destiny, the timeworn, weather-beaten man—who had ridden so long—fell in the rambling grass. I was nearly thirty-one. Assuaged.

I'm perhaps weaker than Pegasus. He was winged. He was the mount of the gods: Zeus, Apollo, Heracles; I was the mount of man or rather a boy set on fire early—a chock full of misery.

. . . And he wasn't my Bellerophon.

You were.

That night under the November moon **327**, when the Persians played the wedding song in their plaintive pipe's . . .

From Memphis to Judea; from Persepolis to Balkh; from Balkh to Badakshan . . . to the very frontiers of Taxila, they are all centaurs, Princess.

In keeping with their nature, just as their human part was incomplete, so too the powers of reason. As men, they despise the arrows because they are harmless; as beasts, incapable of understanding the bedevilment of man. So, they charge, regardless, like drones. Macabre and innocent.

The mares showed us the way as we forward marched from Oxus, the principality of the Amazons, to the Indus and then to the Hydaspes. The campfire and the unrelenting rain. The foals, we had tethered behind.

Hey girl. I finished my education in a hurry. That old Stygrian they called Aristu, was a freak. So damn curious was he, I remember one day in the Nymphian woods of Mieza, he broke a pebble into two. Then one-half he broke again, and so on, to see if there was a speck of gold or a void. In his cave he concocted the potion, for stone was gall in time.

Be that as it may . . .

I'll tell you a fun story, for you wished me a mortal. In our war games when I intuited one side worsted by the other, I dashed off to the winning side and helped them until they were winning again. I laugh and I laugh. In military exercises with the youths, my companion springing on asses by the tombs of the gods, I rode with them. Harnessing mad asses was pure joy, far more a challenge than the broken stallions.

Now I must admit, as you drag me back, had not father tamed the consciously mad colt of the ox-brand with a little hemlock (his terrifying whinny became a ninny), then by Apollo I couldn't've spurred it to be mine. To bridle his unbridle, his groom always mixed hemlock with barley and fodder.

One day I came from behind and kissed pa. He was shaken.

'What do you want sweet son-o-tart?' and he smiled begrudgingly.

'To take part in the Olympic Games.'

'For what event have you been training lad, my donk-willy.'

'Tricycle,' I replied.

'Child, I'll provide you serrated wheels. Contest well; devote your vigor to training, for the event has GREAT PRESTIGE. GO, your body double shall go with you. Bless!'

So, I arrived at the mount. Beside me, Hephaestion lovely—the slow walker of eleven-league fame.

There we encountered Nicolaus of Andreas—king of Acarnania, a boastful man, he conjured the pluck to greet me so, 'Hail, toddler.' I was eleven and he called me thus.

I replied: 'Do not humble yourself so, O king Nico and therefore glory in the assumption that your life will last for eternity, for fate is accustomed to stick on to one place, but the fickle of balance makes mock of the humble man. Much regards.'

'Your thoughts are an aberration. It concerns me baby,' Nicolaus said in indifference. 'You here as a spectator or a competitor?'

'Both,' I replied. 'To compete with you in the tricycle race and to watch you topple.'

'But I shall also be participating as a pancratiast, a boxer, a wrestler,' Nico jested as if to remind me of the versatility of his prowess.

And, I was compelled to reply, 'I've come for the tricycle race. You shall learn from future what is there in the future . . .'

He was touched to the quick, 'See to what a pass Olympic Games have now come,' he whined, he roared and spat at me.

As I had caught a cold, my spittle was thicker, yellowed, rancid.

So the day came. We lined up for the race. The trumpet sounded the fanfare for the start; the standard-bearers signaled to the empty crowd, the starting gates were raised and we burst forth on our pedals.

Nico crashed out first for he was eighty stones. Cimon of Corinth rode back when up a slope. My fiercest opponent Laemodons tires were flayed ribbon. Thanks pop—Thanks your serrated wheels.

. . . And, I decelerated to the finish line.

Crowned with the olive wreath I returned 'ome hearo. Paeans of celebration.

> Thump Philip, Trump Macedonia
> Like the sun on his chariot
> He drove the
> TRICYCLE
> And blotted out all the other stars

> Like father, like son
> Generous king conqueror
> For the olive wreath

> Surely in the spirit of Heracles—the Olympian
> Who proclaimed a gold coin to each of
> His subject with his glorious face imprint

> Proud we are that there be now two glorious
> Face face
> Shining in our raised palms

> Hail glory!!!

It wasn't me he rode when he surveyed the crucified survivors of Tyre. I wasn't there to see the dismemberment of the prince of Gaza. I was hemlocked during the massacre of Branchidae somewhere in central Asia. Blind, blinkered, while Persepolis went up in flames.

Blue moon . . . Blue moon . . .

High . . . high on the Khawak pass—Bactria, the sharp wind whipped my snout. The shiver of your image ripped through me.

He put his face down and covered it with my mane. Hunched and frozen, I looked down the precipice and trotted back.

Night and beautiful by the torches, we slept together in hay. With tender care he embalmed my lacerating hide with an ointment extracted out of a resin of the plant that botanists identify as Sylphion. You shall find it my friends, if you care to—unto this day, in the bazaars of Merv and Bukhara. Even in Lahore, where to this day the mujahedin guerillas use it to heal toxic wounds.

A hundred pillars in the rolling sands. Fifteen Alexandria's, one Bucephela . . . hahhh . . .

*

Syria to Java: To the Moslems, he's a great folk hero. In the Koran Sharif, he a mystery—two-horned, who with his will shall kill Gog and Magog in the teeth of apocalypse.

His choleric rage an icon of what a Man should be.

In the book of Daniel, the 'third beast,' who unleash blood tide.

To the Brachmanas, "mist and earth like *All*"' . . . ONE.

To the Gymnosophists, "'an insect' . . . but not to be trammeled."

. . . *Annata* . . . *Shunyata* . . . to the ephemeral Buddhas.'

Yet fade we all . . . Love evaporate—light and weightless . . . a feather of a golden falcon.

Time is a sea, lapping our feet, bringing back the detritus of froth and corpses. Yet in harvest, the sea part wide, not a desert sand.

331, SUMMER: THE CORRESPONDENCE OF GAUGAMELA

Darius: 'Rest in the lap of your mother. She needs you. You need to play, to be nursed. Accept my humble gift—a whip, a ball, a chest of gold. The whip, that you ought still to be at play; so too the ball. A chestful of gold that you may buy candy.'

Sage was Darius.

'The whip, a hundred lashes. The ball, the world. Gold, the color of spring and desire,' was my reply. 'In the kingdom of exile, O fire worshipper, we shall burn. So my conquests are but bequests to my companion cavalry, to the champions of Isthmus and Olympics . . . To my foot soldiers.'

'Then what is left of you, dear boy?'

HOPE.

*

'O princess, vanity is one sanctuary. Veils of illusion that the Bracmans call a queer call, *Maya* is 'nother.

> *. . . as if birth had never found it*
> *and death could never end it:*

> *. . . the sunlight has never*
> *heard of trees: surrendered self among*
> *unwelcoming forms . . .*

So, would say a poet in the lands beyond the Atlantic. A poet called Archie Ammons. The twain met and unmet. Maverick!

Unwelcoming forms! The avenging deities rack the remorseful.

They have all dwindled to sighs, all feeding on sighs. They're on the moaning hills, the full orb of twilight upon them; pagans, desiccated in the burning miles. That is not the ordinance of Heracles, never *was* . . . Hephaestion!

. . . but don't we flow into each other in bits and pieces? There's a paradox in Ammons. There's a paradox in us.

Yet I yearned: There you were with your musk breath . . . and I don't know, somehow it seems sufficient to see whatever's going and coming is,—but dear princess, I shall not lose myself to the victory of stones and trees, of bending sandpit lakes, crescent round groves of dwarf pine . . .

I pause. You ask me *why*? I'll not demur.

. . . Two hundred leagues beyond there is a deep shade. **INDIA**.

336, MAY 18TH—PELLA

I was well loved, but father had mixed feelings. He half rejoiced in my warlike spirit but grieved, for I did not resemble him in my appearance.

Mother had taken on a new brat called Pausanias. At her behest, he contrived a plan to immortalize father. Father, after beating the Thracians had come home tired and weary. The next morn he visited a theatrical performance. Pausanias was playing Paris but chose to land near Philip by the ex-machina route. Ma came down dressed as Helen. Behind a shroud of drunkenness, he could still identify his wife. Pausanias of the sweet smile delivered a dagger to pa. I was seated by him; the purple hidden in a cloak of white. Pa, thinking he also was a part of the play, stabbed himself. I thought he spilled wine.

The arena was wine and Macedonia mine.

I couldn't stop weeping. Mother laid her hand on my head and immediately the tears dried up.

I was raised to the stilt. I was five-feet six and those buggers were ten a foot.

So, on a stilt I stood and delivered a moving tribute to the spirit of Ares . . .

'This is no country for old men,' I stuttered.

A nerve wind wobbled the stilt. A great sign. So, the flow began.

'Contrary, this is country for old battle-axes and young sling shots; of tridents and tricycles.' That man Aristu was behind me. He imputed what I must say.

'We are the troglodytes, the griffins, the hunchbacked, the hermaphrodites, the satyrs.'

'The king is dead! Short live the king.'

'Every man desires what is better than his own.'

'. . . So to Greece, to Persia, to the eastern seaboard, India, where the world begins . . . . To the end of the world . . . shall we not proceed . . . ?

PEACEABLY

'In peace . . . but men . . . my infantrymen, Hypaspistoi, my friend's, my dear companions Pezetairoi . . . The flaccid is nobler than the erect . . . but you have your pikes, your Sarissa. How long is a Sarissa?'

FIFTEEN FEET.

The uproar was deafening.

When he rode with you as far as the Amu-Darya, he did not mount me. He chose the white stallion they called Plato. It was only after he kissed you a token farewell that I was uncovered of the sheepskin. I saw your retreat, shining like a bronze dream through your burkha. So handsome,

I exhaled blood mist. The icicles around my eyes melted. I sweated steam—sweltering in the icyscape. Hephaestion and Ptolemy were there; a ponderous heat descended on them. The garrison was forlorn.

That winter night when he captured the Sisimithres rock with his lunatic band, it was I who carried the final assault. When he took you for his bride, I bled with Hephaestion.

Why did we bleed!?

May be we knew that you shall banish away his fears. You were ignorant of that particular emotion and he knew it intimately. That was shame. I divined it to be adultery.

And that cost you at the end, like his mother.

. . . Small purchase.

Shall I give you his address, O princess?

The immortals hunt for the mortals. The mortal is the essence in the friable matter.

Every man desires what is better than his own is—the brown and the beautiful.

Have you no graves here to commemorate the dead?
    Where we dwell—the earth
    Dead?
Living or the dead, who are the more numerous?
    Numerous are the dead. Count not the invisible.
    Invisible?
Which is the wickedest of all creatures? Women?
    Far be it!
    Women?
What is kingship?
    Nice day decay
    Kingship?
Which came first night or day?
    Good answer
    Night or day?

Left or right? East or west?
　　　Ask a crab
　　　East or west?
Haven't you a property?
　　　What is proper
　　　Property?
And what is proper?
　　　Flames of a thaumaturge
　　　Proper?
But if we are of like minds the world would be devoid of
activity.
　　　Golden burden
　　　Activity?

And then, I offered Dandamis, the nude Brachman, bread, gold,
wine, my Persian scepter studded with beryl's and diamond, and oil of
the best olive on all earth.

　　　Olive?
　A fruit full of life! I informed
　　　A fruitful bash, I accept.
　　　Fruit . . . life?

And in autumn, leaves dry, *He* struck the fire stone. The precious
oil burned the golden pile of leaves of Ashwatthwa.

So much for the Brachmans! There lay the ford of Hellespont;
the Granicus, the desire for Halicarnassus . . . the oracle of Sibyl; the
Gordian knot. Gaugamela.

DANDAMIS?

Porus is a slave . . . Proceed onto Hyphasis.

323 NIGHT, 9TH OF JUNE, BABYLON

The diadem has dropped off the crest of my helmet. You had seen me
in an iron coronet. A garland of granite wrapped across my waist.

. . . I couldn't stop throwing up and I crawled and crawled to
the beak of a spur overlooking the muddy Euphrates. All star stir in
sky—Crazy diamond in the sapphire blue. But there you were and you
yanked me back just the moment before the plunge.

You thought you saved me from divinity.

DIVINITY.

Is there a star in the sky called Alexandros?

The whelps bark when the dogs cease to . . .

Book 3, chapter 9, Herodotus: *Other Indians, living to the east of these, are Namades, and eat raw flesh. They are called Paedeans. When one of the community is sick, be it man or woman; if it be a woman then the women who are his nearest connection put her to death, alleging that if she be wasted by disease her flesh would be spoilt; but if she denies that she's sick, they, not agreeing with her, kill her and feast upon her.*
Likewise, men to men.
And whoever reaches old age, they do to feast; but few attain to this state, for they put to death, everyone that falls into distemper.

DISTEMPER.

Beautiful indeed . . . Bucephelus
Roxanne, you're in a gold pendant sheltered in a nugget.

Time for the meditative lizards
And the ascetic moths
Bleary demons and blighted nymphs
To grow fat and vanish
In Night's rich harvest

Your lullaby!

Night's harvest! Ah, I say to her. I'd canter home you by the half moon bay. Ride on, dear girl. Your streaming tresses spill through my mane. Ride on my trodden—the moon and morn through the crescent desert sands, Babylon—until we touch the wine flesh of the Trojan: Alexandros Magnificus.

Behind me, there's a wall. The wall has a propensity to crumble. There is mortar; there are cement and plasters—nerves of faith joining it together. O Roxanne . . . I try. Honest I try! The knuckle of my index finger is a dent. It's alien. It's not a parvenu. It's really strong, magnificent beyond the flakes. I'm whole but not near so near. Layers' and layer of prophets are locked, Roxanne. Do I make myself clear, sweet? I wanna' dash through it, but Bucephela is tired. He smirks. The nostrils flare in distemper. When he crossed the Hindu Kush, he neighed soft. Cold, clouds of smoke. High up on the perch. *India ahoy.*

And that bloody horse stooped like a wedged mule. Shame I tame.

I wanna' die Roxanne. I've always wanted to die. Dionysus whisper. The pythons are dead. To see too much doesn't oblige you to see. Token spirits uproot. Ptolemy was wrong and you know it. He could never be a Pharaoh. He could never have taken my place. You could've said so. *Why didn't you?*

The shadow you cast over me is a season's greeting: *Autumn.* Reams of land I roll, are but a cloud of orgy. I know darling, I'm poison in the gall of my birth-star.

Aristu was right. If you come across Socrates in India, then bow low. His thoughts are your deeds, and the trail of causes lead to a cup.

His ugly wart face spoke across the arc. A failed experimenter, he would put me on trial—a darned nonsense. Like the embers, I light in the twilight of drifting snow.

But did I meet Socrates!

I'm enamored. I'm man beyond man. Hephaestion for company . . . oooo! He's dead in Ecbatana. *Without*, can I venture? Indeed, I can—in an unmarked pyramid.

Ptolemy, take me, carry me away to Egypt.

There is lush out there Roxanne. Significant walls to break. Walls, where faith congeal. The arbor, the trellis where we made love.

Love?

Night, day, I think of you. I'm begot.

Roxanne, may I go to meet your maker.

You know when the Persian came to me I was dream fire.

Pompellian wall!

She was man garb.

Roxanne, I thought of you . . .

Of you! *Only.*

You might guess but I thought . . .

Nature is beautiful. Water is water. Earth earth! Aye . . . Air is dream. Fire consume!

Fifteen day I die.

Sorrow me not.

In blood, in hope, I wish I die in your arm. Wishes, dreams.

The wall cannot be breached. There are mortar and marble, lime and plaster: veins of hate and mistrust.

It is memory. They're cutting me up in choice pieces. They are feasting on my liver. Is there enough venom in it left?

Token spirits . . . Huaaaah . . .

AUTUMN.

Reams of sand roll . . . figments of orgy. Darling, you're a prisoner in a star.

I light in the twilight of the Gedrosian sands and drifting flakes of snow in remembrance. Should I yield you?

There is lush out there, Roxanne; significant walls to break. Walls, where faith congeal in wraps of cotton . . .

Elimination of moisture by Natron—that's how they mummify: Ka—the spirit, Ba—the personality, and the Akh—immortality.

The Ka is a simulacrum of the person's spirit. Churned on a potter's wheel by the ram-headed god Khnum, its creation, like wine in an amphora, the body too comes into being . . . like a double— alter-ego, alter-body; now, that it resides in a tomb it has the same needs that nourished us when we were manifest, my friend. May be we reside in each other still . . . what'd'ya say, hey!

The Egyptians leave offerings of bread and date, of myrrh and incense, topaz, ruby, Basreii pearls; they bring along the sun in their papyrus-face, moon-waves in nubile kohl glints, the membrane of broken hymens, in tombs for the Ka to use.

BUT I CREMATED YOU . . . HEPHAESTION.

The Ba is our individuality, our unique character that enters with the breath of life and departs at the time of death. It is free, if it chooses to; it can wander in gay abandon between layers of the underworld and the physical world. It is malleable in space, can take on different forms, despite its inimitable nature.

THE BA IS MY LIVER. IT'S BLEEDING . . . HUNTER.

And then, there is The Akh—that sublime aspect in us that the cannibalistic gods of the underworld would partake; of our flesh, of our blood, our soul—as if they were waiting for an eternity to return back to themselves by devouring their own children. Immortal unchangeable gods, Akh yet is an aspect all in itself—monumental, free-sprung—that loving men create after death by the use of funerary text and spells, deigned to bring forth an Akh. Thus wrapped, with love and in memory, that individual is assured of not 'dying a second time'— a death, that would mean the end of one's existence.

The intact body is an integral part of a person's afterlife, for whence is there a soul without a body and a body without a shadow? For if there be no shadow, there be no name, no Ka, Ba, or Akh. By mummification, the Egyptians believed they were transmuting a successful rebirth in the afterlife.

With the exception of the Akh, all these elements join a person at birth. A person's shadow was always present. *The shadow* must be there. One could not exist without the other; the shadow the halter.

Dream-morphic as they are, for the shadow they represent a small human figure painted completely black.

FOR ME THEY PAINTED A DEER. AN UNKNOWN DEER.

I'm dreaming fire . . . Babylon. Divinity can wait.

All the pyramids of Egypt are commemoratives of man's profound ignorance, Ptolemy. The gods of Homer are dead, the gods of Egypt are dead; of Persia is ash. Bactria is an enclave of fire. We've killed them. We, the marauding hordes, who in the name of the noble Greeks, destroyed ourselves, and everybody who chose to cross our paths.

I can hear the echo of the laughter of the oracle of Apollo at Delphi, the oracle of Sibyl in Libya, the oracle of Jupiter Ammons at Egypt.

The laughter is coming through in waves. Either myopic bastards or ghosts of clear vision.

Gnoyhi seauton: know thyself—they inscribe at the entry to Delphi. A warning to all who fancy they can gain wisdom without knowing the self.

In whose mind did those words arrive? Not through the ex-machina route, of course.

I say some who never were there to know. A stupid oxymoron.

The trail we blazed—we the brigands, the barbarians is our entire legacy. *My* legacy.

At this hour, I feel the kick of hell. I feel like a eunuch; tongues of fire rattle my ribs they put to a toast. I'm a quarrelsome monster, a laughing stock, who only raised a great commotion. To what end, ruler of a crumbling world.

Roxanne, Alexander wouldn't have turned to the west again to face the falling Sun, Had I not reared my head in mutiny. I couldn't go any longer. I was thirty-years eight months. Outlived.

Yet, he was adamant, until the dawn, when the red sun flushed the Hypasis; and he finally had to relent. To my whispers.

His band of brigands lured after talent and talent of gold, power . . . rapine.

Asia looked at my face as we forded the Hellespont. Fools rush in where angels fear to tread and I was mad but not a fool.

There, beyond the Hindu Kush, lay the garden of my becoming. Without me, he was naught. You are the knot in his belly, my sweet rutting Kastouri. You are the navel of perfume I covet. Between the Umbilical and genitals, I hunt the lore of forests. I hunt and I hunt.

The arrow has hit a clutch of the fragrant.

The Kastouri is extinct. You, O princess, I shall keep with me forever. Wear a pendant perhaps. His flesh, I'll sell to a sheik or better to an appointed mujahedeen.

Wishes, dreams, eternity . . .

Poacher Abdullah Bucephelia

THE ESCORT

L et us be together for a while. Make love to me if you like. No, no, no . . . Not right now. Let me get ready first. There may be a few emotional flare-ups but that's par for the course.

Now don't get me wrong. He's a friend alright but he's not me. I'm over and done with this kind of pathology.

My friend did you ask! Interested? Don't be shy. Here I am, google-eyed, no cutt-puss goner. If it doesn't bother you . . . Oh it bothers na? Ok, ok don't run away. Gin madam . . . gin and lime.

Well, he's just one. Happened to be just the softest. There are others more intimate, more profound—so complete in themselves, even I shudder.

Strictly speaking, no; it's just a temporary condition. Ha ha . . . Delirium tremens can wait. It's just the cold. Thank you, you don't have to. It's cashmere, I know. Gin will do for now. Thanks again. I appreciate. You see, *do you see,* any tremor. I can *still*. Tell me about your family. Goner! No girl, you're the heart of it, don't forget. There are beautiful after the twilight.

Death is a part of life, did you say. No girl, where did you come to hear about it, dum. Life is a part of *Life*. I swear by god, I haven't seen a dead in my life. T.V! I don't watch it. Yes, there are images, I know. You don't believe me, do you? I swear by my mother, I've never seen a dead silly.

I'm not there good sis,' you insist on my friend.
. . . Now hy 're you starin' at me. Sorry ma'am staring games are not for me. The self-same game people play. You're not in the same league as theirs, I reckon. 'Nother gin . . . no-no don't worry, I'll pay. Come-on girl, you've tunneled yourself by my friend's gambit. 'Tis foolish. There you hear Baker Street. What I do?

Was into kind of a teaching job. Economic systems! O my, my!! But then I bullied the principal since I took my invigilation duty too seriously. *No breach of conduct while honest students wrote their papers*. You laugh. You make me smile.

But ma'am . . . Some jewels in the bloated tomes could be found before they consign years of insight into the shredder. And those without can wait outside the room.

What a lovely!

Quite! I dashed out, and held in a numb-lock and then by the scruff of the unsuspecting tee-shirt after the mother-fucking obscenity flew inside the classroom. It's urban. Of course you gotta' know that in my lecture, and I smoked, smoked around the classroom, whisper was tabooo . . .

No, not in this hotel. But if you like . . . Dunhill . . .

Friend, the softy. He really was quite the escort: scuttling around lost butts, wandering out and in, into the sublime. Then, this happened. Now shaaa . . . There's no point relating to you what happens to self-guided men when Saturn return.

He took off.

Nothing strange. With middle of the lower middle-class psychos, who learn to teach themselves by reading, and listen small.

He took off.

He was bathing in the river all alone in quaint place, Dharmashala. And click, struuuuh . . . And I, on his behalf, received a photograph day before. Here's it. Wow! Look, look at you. Who's he . . . Some Indian David!

⌒ ⚬⚬⚬ ⌒

He imagined the mislaid butt's: some perky, some so firm, a magic—that's the way of his confide—hanging open, smiling, devouring, cruel, rounded . . . excellent. Shall sag, was his prophecy.

Sag or not, it fetched him decent income. One hundred and fifty rupee, plus single room attached bath plus half whiskey, was his charge. O yes, he too had to call his mother. Every night. Every other night.

⌒ ⚬⚬⚬ ⌒

What she didn't understand—now she was not among the ice-wagon of coal to cream, pardon me—I mean the Franco-Danish thirty something hübsch, was that, you don't call an escort that *'You're a good escort.'* Pray must say, if he's is reasonable good-looking and supple and all other reasonably good-looking guys from this country couldn't have done what he did. For this man knew which party in Denmark her father is a member—exactly which spectrum of the right wing. He also knew how much her ma had to pay to her pa, to secure her the grace of arriving to his territory by the Nord Sea, just to see her male-child once in a piss year. The male child is now a dapper young man and not surprising he's a member; whatever, the painted gray skies and the shale sea—the sister and the brother were light strokes in a Mary Cassatt canvas.

I remember he often used to say about his tribe somewhat green . . . *Illegitimis non carborundum.* By god, I'm perfect sure he knew nit a word Latin. Now my interpretation is that some hum-job did him to envy. But that's just a hum-job and my interprrretation . . .

However, let that be. She's sober, he said. She's gentle and utterly refined, but something strange happens to her—he had paused to tell me that—*yes*, a kind of transformation while she's gist in European congregations.

Not what you're thinking? Are you listening? You do.

I'm wrong; he corrected himself . . . Something strange happens to him. He *becomes* the escort. Take it easy man, I consoled him.

As far as I know my friend wasn't buggered or anything. Now get that straight in. His father never tried so much as to touch him. Men kept a respectable distance. I was an exception. We were friends, and had come equal, when we burned the liquor shop when the MRP did not go down well with us. Arson was a thing that we reviled. Igad!

Men kept a respectable distance. Even noble-bodied Caucasians and the rare Negro—some in the spell of the Taj, some locked in a yoga-knot forever, by the shores of the Malabar or in the *lakangs* of the Buddhas where breath had MRPS. Change for cold comfort.

She was pretty much out of her wits when the old maroon clad nun beckoned him and gave him a crumb of a biscuit. Old nuns always had a crush on him. The time he took a dip in the river Dharmashala, the creased centurion invited him and kissed his forehead, her leather lip before the flash. *Common becoming'—* or something, he said, without an intimation of pride or irony. Well, he had learnt from his erstwhile family that if there be a cake then all shall share it in equal measure. I say some hubris.

He confessed to me that the Dane in her knew it by heart. She got him edelweiss's, two pine leaves or a seashell, she vouched was from the Adriatic. While in his mind there rustled the *trrrrr* of a greenback or a Euro, Yens and a rare Yuan. Hope you understand pound-wise!

You Don't? You are a woman. So, you do. In fact, you must.

Now, he swears his father never raped his mother. Their vanity ran too deep for that. O yes, I remember his pa was a brooding Brando and with a whistle he could kill. Three blocks walk, I never took my mom to my friends' home.

If you don't dig a little dirt sometime you ain't livin'.

Riding on the crest of a wave, far into the skyline of the Puri beach, Bay of Bengal, one lyre-day, he waved his hand to his kid-son and daughter—to his beloved wife and whistled . . .

She nor swooned nor uttered cry. Heavens!

෧ ෨෧ ෨

I often gaze at her letters,

—Their correspondence. He's all but given it to me. In sacred spaces where her voice disappears—between the lines—between the lost verb and the obscure Nordic noun, he often waited.

She too must wait between the Vikings and the sixth republic . . . or is it the seventh, ninth . . . Huhu sweet. It's just eight hours by train from Copenhagen to Paris.

He told her about the dangers that await in India. Don't walk alone at night, they'll whisk you away—they have this thing for white skin and I'll land up in jail. In Indien?? . . . Yes, yes in India. Don't keep dead cats in cell. Don't even try so as to cross the alluring green Ganges even if you fancy you're an Olympic swimmer.

Hehhhy . . . I too don't like dead cats and photographs of it. Sick. SICK. The Brahmins do not like to keep cats. O-kay, okay—Sorry. You do dig dirt sometime.

Well

When in rare moments, she become the lover, her mother talked: I read you a story from *raconte moi une histoire par jour* . . . *L'Oiseau . . . ivre de liberte, sa joie d'etre oiseau et de pouvoir. Voler!* . . .

While I was lost between the call of the forest like a *Samana,* and the intermittent tic of the cicadas—the haunting melody of her seven-year old soul crept into me.

Better time, friend!

Arpeggio rhythms' too many—the separation of her parents when she was sixteen, boarding school—Herlufsholm Kostskole, moved to Toulouse, raped by her French uncle at nineteen. Now, don't blame him if law accede consensual incest.

No ma'am, I don't legislate home good . . . this town scarlet. Tonight all things possible . . . we paint your mother green.

O yes, cross the sky. Yes, we'll celebrate me and you . . . and drink this town dry . . .

My apologies . . .

. . . Learnt to make chocolates in the best chocolatier in Pahii—twelve to thirteen hour non-stretch, six days a week—thirty-five hour workweek—and her ankles gave away. After her incomplete rehabilitation, she sought work in a refrigerator. Four in the morning, she had to wake and got to the ice-cream maker where she met the stick-on pied-noir whose sister got her, her school degree, at the beautiful age of twenty-one tender.

Come to think about it, she's many times a millionaire. I guess so, for I was privy to his ramblings the evening before he refused to breathe.

A flat in Paris, a house in Toulouse, forty acres in Denmark, a quarter to her name, for he had three girl child and a girl extra; quite ho—right wing yet a father. Prime land for sea, sex, solarium.

I have huge work to do on myself—to speak up now as you told me to' I'm slowly reaching that stage. Do speak your mind. Of course it's not funny to stay in your situation. I DO understand. I do what I can to help you. May be I'm not aiming right?

I want us to be free. I felt free with you in India, when alone with you. You gave me the beautiful gift of an orgasm. Believe me you can trust me with your soul and honor that's so damn dear to you.

. . . As I trust you with my fragile soul. I need you.

And he half composed . . . "Don't say a Sea is fragile . . . (*) Some message texting goin' on . . . ooo!

⌒ ✦ ⌒

Now it's a long story. There's the photograph . . . Madam. No, you don't gaze a face you know. I'll tell you more about the story later, as a private investigator.

So long, madam. Hope you're town.

⌒ ✦ ⌒

Ummmm . . . There's a bottle of calcium and 212.5mgs extracts of panax ginseng root, alfalfa tonic. A mirror, which is telling him: Hey mon, you have to go back soon, tone your body soft and dreamy. No, no, it won't do . . . I won't squander it soft. There are Senoritas and Frauleins,' Mademoiselles' and Missus, Shrimoti's, San and Chan . . . all mighty bums. I've to take care of the whole range. Build your pelvic muscles. Squeeze your groin and hold . . . pulsate it . . . hold firm two hours at least. Three you overkill.'

He once showed me a letter and its answer. Today while gazing at his nude photograph, I read it out. It goes like this.

Dearie,

Indeed I am sensitive.

Just like you are.

But we are also more than just that, we can evolve, and people around us will naturally evolve in their own rhythm.

48

We cannot force anything upon them. I cannot force them to follow me. This I must confess.

I implore you. Please, not to be like so many other people are towards me, always with good advice. It's kind of you but I need more from you.

I would like to imagine you to be like a juggler :) but not with my heart :) :)

I do understand that you put huge pressure on yourself. But we are a couple, me hope, na? We should be able to go beyond ourselves; I surely try, leave material matters aside and be fully towards each other. Or am I completely beside the point? Do you feel me wrong, insensitive, lost, stupid, idiot, incoherent . . . . ?

But let us not go pass each other. Let us not miss the point of each other.

I wish to come to be with you, you don't think it's a good idea, I understand. I respect your wish. I hope soon it will be possible for us to be together.

No matter what I, how to say this . . . I feel you deep inside me and forever for having given me a most beautiful present, that of orgasm.

I will never forget what we have together.

Hugs and dance with you that's what I wish.

Ta

His reply; not sent:

This is more than a mail to me. It is a sermon of a life.

I try best not to force anything on anyone but by nature, I'm forceful. I cannot help and I do wish to learn.

I'm not talking about sex.

I cannot see anybody die. In this short span since childhood, I have consciously and unconsciously brought back many from the dead zone. Now I am dying, a world is fading away and I have to fight my own battle.

I never juggled with anyone's heart.

Yet your hotel room words struck me deep down my soul. For the first time going back home in a bus, I broke down completely; felt desolated. The sympathy of common people—co-passengers got me back home. My thanks to the driver.

You are not stupid or incoherent or lost and I do not blame you but Ahab-like bitterness has set in.

In one simple stroke you took away the blaze. Since then, I've tried to keep my cool, trying my very best to unremember.

Our point, *my* point has been set adrift.

It could only have been done by a woman like you, with your faith, beauty and honesty. None else.

Do not apologize.

I have to get out of this negative feeling or else I'll suffer. I'm in a very high point of sadness. Call it depression.

Intense self-hate and physical revulsion, a complete brooder—now my soul trembles with fear and loneliness. I walk around the streets and the stadium but I get no consolation from nature.

It was good that a child wasn't there. He would have gone straight to hell.

This I rant.

Time to time, I'll keep you update on my progress. How far I've been able to lift myself; if the sense of inner joy has resurfaced—that joy, which took me above heaven since childhood to thirty-three.

෩ ༖ ෨

The language of her call seared through me not for the delicacy, the muslin spirit, but as a friend, I knew the drift was *his*. He used to write just like this to her. Other letters I shuffled corroborated the point.

His reaction, his reply stuns me. He seemed fraught: a shameless betrayal of what we stood for despite the arson. What could she have said in the hotel room by the rail station, New Delhi? He just went there to bring her to his home. This too, I know for I accompanied him to the junction. He said he might be late.

Now it's a long story as I said and I could drag on. To you my friends . . . I say . . . Illegitimis non carborundom . . . don't let the bastards wear you down.

Spare a thought for the bastards out there in the meanwhile.

Love love.

If the hat is frayed softie, try your father's.

LITTLE GREEN POOL

I lived in an island for long time.

I lived in a green pool.

I've had dalliances with society now and then. One needs a certain exchange, a conduit—a passage. I do not and swear I utterly, I do not despise them. For it was time . . . and now . . . I begin to believe that their opinion and assessment are now mine, likewise by some wise design whereby we may secure a safe return to our home: to our children.

Now there, I remember the sweet bridal chant, the braid of golden bays entwined in soft resplendent locks—the loveliness of the lulling wedding lay; but when the arrow discharged, nothing could've resisted—neither shield nor breastplate nor any strong defense, if such there be.

There was a time I maintained a body of mercenaries. I had a dappled little guinea pig for company, a canary, a toad. Their ranks swelled and as I poured libations to the heroes, there was a kind of mutiny. They burned their cities yet built temples to earth, air and water. So, I said goodbye to teem of temples and was delivered like an abandoned ship, by waves, to my small island.

I lived in a green pool . . .

Ere . . . I lived in that island. A bountiful one too. At night fall, I lite up fires, as I was wont to do at other times. And, in the quaver light, I found myself tethered; a portion of me I must have left behind. I saw faces: the tutting toad and the mush of the guinea pig and other sort of claims. I only retained a fountain of saliva.

. . . The green pool I live . . .

Now saliva is the sea—that blue-yellowed monster—and I, a sentinel. That island sea . . . a lemon-green fog, like a tower in the night. A beacon of vast abundance. Super cool. Island in an inlet of a stream—the beacon of vast abandoned hope.

I thought I must've seduced.

I was far too advanced in years and so they sent me their embassy. They came with magi-like gifts in the colony of my dark.
I seized them with hunger. After all, I had and have a claim on the gifts, my haughty tyranny, my savage violence, notwithstanding.

Nevertheless, I was the satrap in former days and gifts are due like solemn oaths.
This day, as I belch smog, they delve for my body and disperse it far and wide and I'm the scatter of the little greenish pools where they make a home, they alight for a while; make dance, swim, scatter . . .
Strangers' all. A body of mercenaries . . . Ah!

Requiem To A Marine Snail

In spite of anything that one may hold against her, it must be said that she was gracious enough not to let him feel like a monkey. She knew he had a face too—not a human one—but not of a chimpanzee either. For some strange reasons, *he* wore dark goggles even under the spotlight.

One could see that when she spoke, she held her head with nobly mannered ease and the expression on her was not unlike a mannequin. Goddess!

Her high cheekbones cast a strong shadow right up to the arc of her jaws. Freckled steel eyes. Raven plaits tied up in a coiffure. A single line jutted out of the corners of her asymmetric, retroussé nose and tantalized close up her lips—which she swiped intermittently with the tip of her tongue. A cultivated sort of delicacy that *I* could see he adored.

He strived to answer to her questions in the erudite manner befitting a well-known economic analyst with a knack for eastern affairs, especially of India and China. The recessionary forces assailing the world and how it was different in its causal trajectory that had led to the great depression and the more recent crises—East Asia, Bolivia, Argentina, Japan, Greece . . . Ireland; the likelihood of beggar-thy-neighbor domino, and other such insights, which required of a crisp wit.

Persuasion political . . . ?
    O no, none.

Never mind none . . . Do'ya imagine socialism exist?
    'A retreat of shadows so full that she would sow a thousand sonnets in men's soul,' said Baudelaire. I tend to think they're wearing a thousand bonnets.

Which stage of capitalism . . . *?*
Long-run Keynesian full-employment equilibrium.

Monism?
Drape 'round . . . seep wondrous like a geisha.

Antithesis?
Thesis is the sacred function of a lullaby.

Spiritualized?
Yeeee . . . na na na! If one is a fan of one's own karmic foible, then that poor fan—he can be exonerated to the extent that he has struck the Narcissus in him. Those who have selective amnesia may be completely exonerated. Neither a lucid stripe nor a seascape . . .

Unlike the erstwhile, where tyrannical concord comforted us for toil . . . No another exist, nor even the possibility . . . of 'nother. Expect *luminous* escape . . . .

It was indeed informative, yet I had the curious feel that he was answering to her lips and his nostrils flared as if to suck in the charmed air. She was dragging him to a trench yet not quite pushing him over; she interjected and put in a number of caveats to his argument, which neither spurred nor deflated him unconscionably. How the optimist isn't learning French; *le pessimiste d'aucun voie un chinoise.* That is . . . between the commercial breaks.

What's the impact of recession on masses?
Hummm—cinema and facebook! Wagon or frigate, carry me away.

Which phase of the politico-business cycle?
Dilating and astringent with each beat—blue slate vapor.

How do think immigrants are going to inform policy?
Cinema, hip-hop and the quaint zebra-crossing . . . *If* they ain't rockin' the Kasbah.

The need to under-write welfare state?
Economic Darwinism . . . Milady.

Darwin . . . how many adjectives to him?
  Bangin' on the bongoes like a chim . . . pan . . . zeeeee.

So you think a giraffe can reach the tree top coz it made an effort? ´
  Possible, if ancient sphinx meets souls angelical.

The science of mutation?
  NO NO, no no . . . I don't mean to say the intellectual or the scientific edifice is wrong. I'm no mafia . . . contrary . . . no fasista either . . . peace peace . . .

Credit society . . . ?
  The Goodluck society.

. . . Unemploy' on the increase?
  Agreed, pap's I can't see.

Your long-run full-employment equilibrium? But . . . the hunger in third world, Monsieur?
  Nutrition-experts are singing paeans about the health value of insects, especially roaches.
  However, it was obvious that he was dragged to the very limits of his acquired knowledge. I did not fail to notice that he wasn't economizing with time and she often reminded him of that with an admonishing flutter of her false eyelashes.

Demand sluggish . . . ?
  Yogic fifty percent . . . Domestic demand isn't sluggish. Karma-Nirvana syndrome.

All right, but talking about a country like India, suppose, the economic survey says that domestic demand is an all-time high. How is it possible if you say hunger—which I construe to be poverty—pardon me if I am mistaken, is so wide spread?
  Which economic survey, World Bank or the Indian government?

I just chanced to have a glance on the economic survey published by the ministry of economic affairs, India.

O, I see. Thou, who consoling frail mankind in pain—taught us to make our guns and gun-cotton.

Not all empirical data are brewed like rabbits in hats?

Agreed, valiant efforts are made. I mean if you are conducting sample survey, then you have to prepare a questionnaire, which one *can* read. You can't put a hat on a rabbit. Or maybe, you can, strap it 'round with an elastic. So cute!

The specter of a slump? But I can't help see no, forgive me for intervening; prices ain't fallin'. The relative price of primary products contrasted with industrial products is on the rise, whereas the contrary state means a real slump?

That's a fantastic definition of a slump . . . Old Oxford?

Can the China-model work for India? I mean the economic variant. These two countries are the emerging giants?

Great cathedral-like you frighten me. The dragon is belching sulphur; if you insert a suppository, you get larger eggs. The reverse vegetarians react after a lag, a long lag: I mean the engineers, must first come back home . . . isn't it? Once I did go there for a conference of aubergine delicacies and the queue by the United States embassy and other such countries were like fifty-miles long. I also met quite a few who have given up their jobs in respectable public sectors and swiping windscreens in Toronto.

Pakistan?

Folie à deux. The intelligence service sector is very strong. Put money where the mouth is. F-19'S. All Omar Khayyams.

Okay . . . The left-leaning polymaths seem to think something's very wrong while the right leaning . . .

They lean on each other. Talking about left or right polymaths, they sure possess the economic wherewithal to buy an extra telomere length . . . . else, how can they wimple off their jargons. They are fully employed.

And what is your contribution apart from the rhetoric, Mister—?

Patrician? Temporal lobe epilepsy.

It was pleasure talking to you.

Thank you, the pleasure is mine.

You've been briefed. Afghanistan, Polanski . . . an hour and thirty sec's to go—football fans . . . SOUTH AFRICA—great country . . . much to come after the break.

Many thanks, monsieur economisté.

☙ ✺ ❧

Later they discussed about it—the camera and the general crew got together and gossiped over glasses of beer. A thin old scrawny make-up artiste suddenly remarked, *'She knows all the answers!'*

'She does!?' exclaimed a young recruit in mock surprise.

'And these days, ugh . . . a bunch of assholes . . . third rate,' the old man paused and sighed. 'Are only called upon to fill in the slots. The chair where those pundits used to sit, the dwarfs do these days. All laced.'

'Cuum'on old man. Where are your puuudits's now?'

'Turning in the graves . . . snot-nose! All turning. These peddlers . . . shaaa! The true oracles, all dead.'

He hissed out the last words, an air of finality.

'. . . Make her up less so like a whore, dear rattlebrain'— One light crew patted him. 'The orals would crawl out of their graves if they saw such a chick. Old fella' ha'bout a felllatio 'ey!'

'She no whore Charlie' the ancient makeup man winced as if he's stabbed. 'She knows . . . she knows . . .

☙ ✺ ❧

Two candidates in prime time were fighting over a lost cause and none of them could bring themselves to come upon a solution—to undeceive the other. The electorate is un-split but hadn't a choice; rationality isn't a given; no one wishes to settle for the second-best—but in the end the random run of neurotransmitters shall determine.

These are the slices of reflection that she had scribbled in her spiral-leather-bound diary. O yes . . . she had some education for sure.

I knew, she had that singular acumen of a mass communicator. She had the looks; she could hold sway over the audience with her sheer sense of timing; could see things in perspective; strike up a dialogue with any fucking moron and hover toward some semblance of truth or a general idea in her mystified Socratic way. I never once saw her reduce a man to a pulp. She only wiped a few layers of poultice but never staunched an ego. More significant, I reckon, was her disarming chutzpah or *controlled gall* should I say? No wonder she had leapfrogged from a newscaster to a hard talking celebrity interviewer in a two-year stint—an accomplishment, which many her age could fain hope to achieve.

I was watching the secret life of marine snails on the BBC or Discovery or some other pro-biotic show. Petropods—they call them; have translucent bodies, that you can see it all.

More surprisingly, they mimicked many of the pathways of human intelligence, like for example storage and retrieval of data; learning from experience etc. Scientists are striving to *know us through them.* Imagine that!

It was truly an adorable program—beautifully made and intelligible. I remembered a documentary about penguins (probably a French production) and for a few days, I felt sub-human.

I had taken an aspirin or a sleeping pill, perhaps laudanum and laying on the couch my mind drifted to fey ideas on evolution and becoming. Then the remote switched to channel thirty-three and I saw myself on a midnight retrospect.

I looked like an artichoke; she like a deity and a throbbing, choking lump came in on me. I began to throw up and grope for her diary. *Don't hide away from me: You can escape the sunlight—you can't escape the dark.*

Yet a few afternoons later, there I was *wondering*, when I brought those flowers to the cemetery by the promenade—where the subdued din of the swirling ocean could be heard—if I did the right thing in turning her into a marine snail.

OF LOVE AND TRUTH

The protagonist Kamal ponders over the nature of truth in Naguib Mahfouz's timeless classic on Cairo.

He reflects, '. . . *For truth was as beloved as flirtatious, inaccessible and coquettish as any human sweetheart. It stirred up doubts and jealousy, awakening a violent desire in people to possess it and to merge with it . . . like a human lover; it seems prone to whims, passions and disguises. Frequently it is cunning, deceitful, harsh and proud . . .*[1].'

The ardent Kamal's courtship with truth stems from the bitterness of unrequited love. Truth becomes a beguiling substitute, a personification of the attributes of his theanthropic muse.

We too, the ardent and the not-so-ardent, often have to go through such a rite of passage (not necessarily love), such quirk of events that provokes us to wonder about truth, among other things.

Being sentient creatures, we are pervaded by an aesthetic self-consciousness; we seek to explore the apparently paradoxical and ambiguous nature of reality. Appearances can be deceitful and reality elusive, just like Kamal's muse.

Is truth determined by a mere plebiscite of facts, as the empiricists would like us to believe? Of course, facts may be manifest or not manifest. Is truth a consensus, an agreement on reality, reached in the context of an open discourse?

The notional definitions of truth are laden with assumptions, presuppositions and perceptions, which we bring to bear upon it, as post-empiricists contend!

Pari passu, is love an instinctive bio-chemical ritual?

Is it a learned behavior, an agreement on its nature reached in the context of social discourse? Is it laden with preconceived ideas?

Must we not ask ourselves what we seek?

It seems eminently plausible that the pursuit of both love and truth has an evolutionary role for mankind. It enables us to create, to regenerate—to survive. Yet the individual, who dares dwell on such issues, may be blighted by cruel and unsettling doubts and dilemmas.

Naguib writes on Kamal, '. . . *He seemed to believe that truth would always be cruel. Should he adopt the avoidance of truth as his creed?[2]*'

Is there a choice here, or even the necessity of one? Endless questions arise. We flounder in desultory turmoil. The answers like truth and love, flirt with us; move beyond our grasp like a wily enchantress: like the brilliant flashes of a gossamer sensuousness it allures us, drag us into infinite regress. We lose ourselves in the labyrinth of delusions.

The rapture may renege; the infatuation may turn into an existential angst. Should we then hoist this burden and totter on?

Kamal reflects, '*The problem is not that truth is harsh, but liberation from ignorance is as painful as being born. Run after truth until you are breathless. Accept the pain involved in recreating yourself afresh. These ideas will take a lifetime to comprehend, a hard one interspersed with drunken moments . . .[3]*'

Once he had reflected on love, '. . . *I don't understand its essence and I know nothing comparable. I often wonder if it's not the shadow of a much greater magic concealed within her . . .[4]*'

. . . It seemed as if he were speaking about truth!

I didn't ask her name. Her name doesn't matter. Her voice so merrily chimes . . . her eyes twinkle like a star.

She is a songsmith. Indeed, she is, but I like to think she is Tara . . .

TARA

Five mango leaves
And a pitcher of water
I do not know
If you really sprinkled water over me
I do not know
If you really wetted me or
Not
But you made me a prisoner for life[5]

As the palm liquor coursed through her veins, she thought of Eka. Last night, under the crooked boughs of a flowering mango tree, by the alluvion banks of the stream, they had made love. Their bodies had burned with ardor, and even squalls of a marauding wind that brought in its fray the cool wetness of the stream could not break the swell of desire!

By the same embankments, she had once come upon the *Shramana*. She had filled up a pitcher of water and was on her way to her jungle hovel. Night birds were flying in across the stream to roost in the branches of the forest. She had reached as far as the mango tree when a soft white apparition of a man hailed her, 'Which trail leads to the cave, oh woman?' he asked in a serene voice.

'Is our great father you seek?' she inquired.

His eyes were cast down, and he seemed to gaze at his feet.

'I wish to meet the materialist sage Ajita Keshakambalin—one who is wrapped in a blanket of hair,' he replied.

She was a little mystified by his humility. She put the pitcher down under the mango tree and made as if to go along with him and show him the way. Water had dribbled out from the pitcher and drenched the thin spread of the cloth she wore, but his eyes weren't watching her.

'. . . No, oh kind woman . . . do not bother so. Just point to me the way.'

'Oh!' she sighed, a trifle affronted by what she construed to be a genteel rebuff; she pointed out to a cattle track on her left and said, 'The trail here leads to a mulberry bush and then the track disappears. From there, you can see the head of an outcrop. Wait until the evening star crowns the head and then observe the wind. It won't be a flickering one. It would blow steadily in one direction . . .'

The Shramana raised his head and saw her face while she was still speaking. Now she cast her eyes low and continued, 'Proceed leeward to the wind. Move as the cattle moves until the star is at an arms gulf from the outcrop. Then you shall come upon the shack of Eka. Call out his name. He should be at his place at this hour, and he shall lead you to the den of our sage.'

'Woman, shall you not also give me the direction of heaven,' he said in faint satire and smiled ironically. And he whispered inwardly, '. . . *And who shall steer me across time?*'

She laughed at his persiflage. Her voice rang merrily like the chime of bells and she gave him a frond of five mango leaves.

'Carry them with you,' she said. 'They pick up the wind well. And beat them on your palms as you go along. It shall ward off the animals.'

'. . . And what about the serpents?' he mocked lightly, in an impish voice, assuming the cadence of an adolescent.

'They stay off the tracks,' she answered.

. . . Why so!

'They are tamed by the venom of Eka.'

'Aye . . . I see,' he exclaimed and he held up the pitcher for her.

Oh! Do not bother so . . . ,' she said puckishly like a nymph. 'And hurry. Run like a deer . . . for the star and the wind do not relent.'

'Yes, indeed,' he uttered comprehendingly. '*Indeed*, kind lady . . . the star is climbing fast.'

Then he walked briskly along the leeward trail and disappeared beneath the empurpled foliage of teak trees.

His image held on to her. His feet had the soft whiteness of a lotus petal and the star was in his eyes.

. . . And the Aquarian air flirted with her senses

☙ ✣ ❧

She was Tara—the darling of the materialist seer. Their abode was a cave, deep within the forest, on the outskirts of Kasi. A mist was rising from the gentle river whose course skirted the edge of the primal woods; and while strands of the mist were getting entangled in the thickets and the confused foliage of tree tops, the Shramana, under the fig tree, for a fleeting while, thought of the deep woods ahoy . . .

> The night dew of the sky
> Does not exist
> With the rising of the sun
> Likewise after death
> The earthly body of man
> Mixes with the earth[6]

As the night grew old, her heart began to tremble with gloomy misgivings. She looked at the blind savage.

'How many blind men are there in this universe?' she thought.

The ancient man muttered something to himself and clenched his fists and shifted his weight backward to the dark walls for support. Then he let out a remorseful sigh and kept mumbling inwardly in a trance. His encumbered head rocked very slowly as if lulled by a song. As he moved, a giant shadow flickered on the walls of the cave. Silhouetted by the light of the lamps, the humongous head swayed like a moving mountain. Everything seemed tiny and insignificant by contrast. An indecipherable drone issued from him.

'I can hear you great father. The day you said so, I believed in you. Perhaps I would have believed in the same things, even had you not come.' Tara brooded silently and took a deep swig of the palm liquor that the abstemious sage had so thoughtfully laid aside for them; she flinched in sullen apprehensions and her upper lips twitched involuntarily.

'The whole world is dancing like a restless flame, and you sit there and delve into the dark inertia of your material soul. All our lives we sit and hear the same things over and over again but do you hear a *different* music, father?'

. . . Or is it the song of darkness!

The brew has been perfect. The liquor is suffusing me like the mist through the cave. Yet why do I hear your song of darkness and your call of earthly return?

When you kicked your son, you hit him right at the core . . . where dwells the spirit and yet you refute it!

The footsteps of the Shramana on the wet white sands of the silver stream had disappeared the day after, but he has left his footprints in me . . . and you deny of its existence!

I felt the warm wetness of Eka's skin even as he's beyond the forest, and may never return . . . . and you deny it!

Yet why did I believe in you when I first heard you, as if it was in me, *always* inside—and you just awakened it with your magic touch.

Magic!

. . . To be born and to die as water.

Your doleful words carry the refrain of darkness and isolation and I yet believed in you . . .

And now echoes of all things turn blue in minds crystals, like Eka's blue crystals of death . . . .

. . . But, O sage, tears aren't water, and of course, you can't deny that?

Tara looked at Kali and thought: when the palm liquor swirls in our spirit; we leave the cares aside and forget the yield of our labors. We leave our cares aside, and mock our means and hoist our dreams and dance to the songs of the earth; and thus we travel for miles . . . . And the miles we travel at great speed converge in a mustard stalk, and the yellow sap would mimic the amber light of the moon and the fathomless columns of gold and cinnabar. Then the plants shed their leaves, the flowers dry up, and so do we rest in dream fatigue. Our men, so redolent of sweat and blood, come back to our bosom and make love to us. The same men: poison men and diffident assassins, furtively drift to the snares of gilded cities. Men so sweet and shy that they cower as we shout at them and do as we bid them to do; the very men shall kill with their venom darts . . . and may even breathe heaven in the tinsel taverns. But shall they not spare a thought for us. Shall they not return to their jungle homes?

Oh our men!

So like children they are; their wan breast free of conjectures, their pacific minds never becalmed; their wounds turn septic. Men of earth and fire, baptized by the gall of ancient honor and retribution . . .

Kali gazed at Tara and a dark foreboding crossed her mind, too.

Oh Tara, she thought in deep anguish. You sing for the man, you sing for all of us. Your song is the song of our jungle . . . is the song of our remorse and our battle song too.

. . . Tara, you so touched by grace, brew up songs like our heady liquor. How you weave your rosary of words! Yet I can see a string of anguish and desire coursing through you . . . taking you away to the forbidden heavens of fugitive passions from the dead weight of broodings . . . A liquefaction of matter! And there you find your refuge . . . But what shall become us?

When the corpses of our men drift with the waters . . . and they shall have redeemed their pledge with blood and spirit; but our children will listen to your song of love and soil; and will play with clay figurines and hunt with cane bows and their teeth shall dazzle like pearls when they smile so delightfully, with the moon in their hearts and fowls in their belly—and like little prince and princess they shall court each other with feather and flowers tucked to their tiny ears and dusty hair and will run back to us when they are hungry. And while we wipe off the grime from their faces, we'll tell them the tale of their fathers and lull them to sleep with your songs . . .

෧ ෴ ෨

Take me to the river
Show me the way
Steer me through time
Touch my lips
Blow off the light
Hold my arms
Kiss my body
Show me the way

Her haunches ached with fatigue, and resting her head on her arms, she drifted off into a stupor. There she met the Shramana once again!

He emerged from a mantle of mist but she couldn't see the whole of his face. In fact, she had been thinking of the Shramana all the while, but when he emerged from the discreet white veil, she wasn't able to identify him at first. An inner voice warned her not to recognize, and in obedience to that bidding, she feigned unfamiliarity. Slowly she urged the inner voice to recede and it reluctantly gave way to her wish. For a moment, the Shramana gained enough ground to draw her full attention. His eyes were cast down, and yet another set of the same eyes seemed to be watching her with desire but from beyond the stream. There was a gulf of water between them and she waded across. She was drenched up to her hips and saw his tremulous milky feet in the water. His face dissolved again and she heard a deep moan issuing from somewhere. She saw that she was in conflict. She tried to recreate the face and trace the voice at the same time. Swirls of water gushed through her. The moan became deeper like the monotonous drone of the rushing water.

Woman, shall you not steer me through time?

She tried to mould the face from the clay of his voice. The anguished drone was tugging at her attention, while she clutched onto the image that played hide and seek with her senses and was stirring the deep sap in her. For an instant, she saw the profile of his countenance in the darkening shade and his eyes caught the glint of planetary lights.

She heeded to *his* inner voice now; that was forbidding him to touch her. He raised his left hand imperceptibly and his beautiful long fingers ached in her direction for a lingering while, and then they arced back grudgingly and his hands fell limp along his flanks. He half-closed his languid eyes and his lips parted ever so slightly. For a tantalizing instant, she urged the image to stroke her body. She struggled to wish away the inner voices that was encroaching the zone of hazel light between her and her gratification. For a moment, she succeeded in pushing them far back in her mind's recesses.

. . . And in that magical ephemera he touched her lips and she tasted the fragrance of his breath; and he held her arms and savored her nipples and kissed her down; and then further down to her navel . . . and the moist wisps of desire.

. . . And then, the apparition dissolved as the Shramana waded beyond the alabaster mist.

THE BLIGHTED ASTROLOGER

This is a story told to me by a shrine-keeper in the mist-covered village of Laolin, China. Over the fumes of an ancient pipe—across the veil of time—and we became friends. His lyricism was touching; his language a parable. What I couldn't understand, I divined, for like him, I too was a drifter and therefore we glided together. Being an authoress, I consider it my sacred duty to convey to you, my friend, the basic design and patterns that evolved in my mind without taking recourse to falsehood and fabrication. That is easy. Far difficult was to translate the idiom into an alien tongue, which in this case is English. I scribbled down on bits of paper, the tale of a man (an astrologer of remote past) around whom his rendering mainly circulated. Things of a more contemporary and secular nature, we discussed as well, but I thought it not pertinent to drag them here. Like decaying orbits, he lapsed into mumbling and at times total silence prevailed. As you know, it is best to contemplate during those quiet spells . . .

Every time he ponders over the causes, he discovers that the cause itself has changed. It is emblematic of the memory he keeps—memory, like an unguarded sanctuary—a forest of broken mirrors and failed prophecies. When he gazes at the withering stalk of jasmine, now a streaked gray, he could recall in perfect clarity, the nubile white blossom it was just eleven days back. The fragrance hung like a halo in the interstices of his mind. Foggy-eyed now, he looked at the fading blossoms and the waft of a different time fanned the residual fire in him: *'She almost always wore jasmine in her coiffure. Everything is a phantasm—migrant perfume of a distant land.'*

He wasn't sure even to this day, whether the tresses which kissed the flowers had touched him? Or, was it he who had failed to reach out to grasp the gossamer.

Traveling deep back in time, the decrepit old farmer reached the erudite corridors of the University of Nalanda—where he had been a student of astrology and cosmogony—carrying a manuscript which he had painstakingly transcribed in Chinese in the year when the unremitting drought brought men nearer to his last mask.

It was the zodiacal year 1243 C.E. Only a few students had been able to survive the meager ration of cereals that the adjoining villages had supplied as tithes to the university a year before. In fact, there was only just a few students—fifteen if his memory served right; seven to be the exact count when he left,— under the tutelage of the tottering ninety-five year old abbot Rahula Sribhadra, who kept on going as if he had forgotten to die.

Pu-Li's shoulders hung low. Out of the three novitiates who had made their way through the seventeen years of rigor, he was the brightest. Seventeen years he was sure, for he had mastered how to mark time to its minutest second even though time was recorded here in a *water-clock*. 'Water clock indeed,' he sniggered. His shoulders hung low—his face a death mask—he had failed to predict the year when the clouds would disappear from the horizon in spite of the telltale signs of flourishing acacias and the flame-of-forest trees whose bloom was a despondent ochre. For a while, he paused; he cast a diffident eye on the bow-marked floor of the *viharas* and the scalded parabola of the *Sariputta stupa*.

While he snaked his way through the labyrinthine alley's that led to his cell, he wondered, Why? His data were irrefutable: the great malefics' were in their respective houses, the dragon's head Rahu was annulled by three powerful benefics', each seven houses from its own and the houses cohabited in cozy quadrant from the ascendant. He had crosschecked. He worked his way by regressing back from the lunar constellations—the *Nakshtras* to the sidereal alignments—calculated the nodes to an approximation of an insignificant point-two degrees, and he was sure as spittle in his dry mouth, that his reckoning was incontrovertible.

'The debacle is an aberration,' he muttered, rasping under his breath. The red-bricked walls of the hoary half-burnt institution laughed down on him and for a moment, it had become profane. Profane, and an extension of detached shadows—of decapitated masters and priors. Even half a century of rain could not wipe out the soot that clung on to the walls. The three month long conflagration that had raged when the marauding hordes of the *Ghurid, Bhaktiyar Khalji* burned the library—and the flotsam embers of the manuscripts still drifted, limpid and frail, like so many ravaged wings.

Fifty years!

The drought had come through in waves. First as a tremble in the distant fields, it had come closer surreptitiously, invaded the atmosphere, caused a wrinkle in the brow of the low undulating hills and then began to rape the very earth, which gaped and gaped and consumed the bodies of tillers and animals—drying up the milk in the breasts of mothers. A few emaciated cows foraged on desiccated, but now toxic shrubbery in a desperate bid to survive; the mongrels lapped up the thickening marrow; a silence once ominous, now a pure drone of matter filled up the spaces and time came to a flustering halt. Gatekeepers had drunk up the waters from the water-clocks.

'Yes' he nodded grudgingly. Yes, the cat did not claw the ground; he had seen no cloud draped in a peacock's hue, no blue hills on the horizon. No moon, like the eyes of a dove. He had not noticed a chameleon's stupid upturned gaze, and the heifer did not hasten back to her calf in the days preceding the drought.

Pu-Li had not opened his eyes to nature. He had seen a rainbow full and tactile—a skein of geese flying ninety degrees anti-clock to it—back to his homeland. Now he shuddered in dismay as he reminisced that the direction of the sky where the rainbow hung was east—a certain sign of drought. *Too late'*—It has all become a prodigious mistake.

Nature wasn't lying, but neither were his calculations! The Jupiter was not at perihelion and had not made ingress into Capricorn; far from it. The air was enchanting, not to say laden with a sweet moistness—at least in his cell and in her presence . . .

Venus was transiting close to Pleiades in the house of the bull and the red moon wasn't anywhere near the asterism of Rohini or his Pi of

Sieu. Agreed, the sun was in conjunct with Venus but was aspected by the austere and ascetic Saturn.

Not even the great masters could deny that.

'Then what went wrong?'

'Was the immense evocative sky not a part of the cosmic principle that dwells on the crust of mother earth; the animals and birds, the vegetation and the colors that play around, merely did so to deceive him—Pu-Li. Were the venerable principles of astrology a mere sham—a surrogate for ignorance—or has the very earth detached itself from the astral forces that had bound it for the infinity of time past and is now a free orb, moving on its own rhythm?'

A limpid sadness pervaded Li. What brought him to India was not the lure of the knowledge of a people of a different race—that is no gulf at all—but the fact that he met himself at the point of departure.

One day, when happenstance, he looked at his reflection in the tremulous waters of the 'Lu-shi-kang' lake where a "thousand jewels shine," he saw a single ripple, where his eyes shone a moment like two drops of pearl and the image drifted southward. The boatman had smiled as he followed young Li's gaze. The ripple gathered mass and lashed at the distant gravelly banks beyond which lay the barrier of the mountains of eternal snow.

Even then, he was well known all around the countryside as a sign reader and had been invited to the royal court of the Southern Sung dynasty, as an apprentice oracle. He had demurred. He knew that the mandarins would treat him like a jester for the amusement of their concubine's, even while taking credit for the rational analysis and forecasting of impending future conditions. Those lackeys of the sovereign would usurp his magic eye to curry favor with the emperor. And why should he? —He knew by meditating on the nature of events, that it was just a brief interlude of peace before the Mongol Tartar hordes would ravage his land once again. His imminent departure for the capital was bemoaned and anticipated, with not an unmixed joy, by his poor mother since he was her only child.

Yet the swathe of water that mirrored his eyes, he *must* follow. To him it was a new sign—a passage. He had been a nature reader, a gift that manifested the moment he could communicate. Like a cat, like a chameleon, like a water-hog, a serpent, a beetle, he anticipated events and conveyed them by gesticulations and grunts as a child, by clear communication as he learnt to speak. Seldom was he wrong, whether it be a hailstorm or an earthquake, a flood or a deluge.

Droughts never occurred in the village (nobody could call to mind such an occurrence) he grew up, but then drought was just the inverted image of ciphers that portended seasonal downpours, that brought in its wake splendid harvest or floods.

Most times, he couldn't see the sky, for the vault of heaven was covered in a kind of perpetual mist. From hearsay, and then a yearning to walk the path of Xuanzang, in the blazing sun, torrid deserts, exotic tropical plains and clear nights took hesitant roots in his veins. The two droplets of pearl that became a single flash of silver line as it broke the shore, was the augury he was looking for. He decided to leave for India.

From a Nature Reader he had become a reader of the sky, as though the sky was not nature, as if an invisible wall divided the sentient earthly appearances from the astral configurations the heavens above.

At Nalanda, under the auspices of the ageing patriarch Rahula Sribhadra, and his guidance and references to scattered teachers thereabouts, he had learned through great effort, diligence and will, Sanskrit and Pali, the sacred treatises of Pancha-Siddhantika of Varahamihira and Brihat Parashara Hora-Shastra, Saravali by Kalyanavarman, and a hundred other texts harking back to the time of the Greek incursions—Yavanesvara and remoter still, the Brihat-Samhita, with palpable Indo-Greek influences. He had translated them to Chinese that he may trace the destiny of his countrymen and his country and the unfolding of events.

The drought had shattered his confidence. For the last time he entered his cell, packed his austere belongings; cast a longing glance at the rice-bran bed where he had made love so many a blossom night to the bronze hued village girl, Sukhavati.

Sukhavati was the daughter of the local Brahmin, who took upon himself to support the old teacher in deference to a fading cornucopia of insights. Li called her Su-ko-ti. *So fond* of her was he! She too found his eyes, his earlobes, his cuticles extremely cute. That he guessed when she gawked adorably on those finer points in his otherwise rustic mien. Furthermore and of greater significance, he thought she was disarmed by his mercurial intellect. It was easy to stow her discreetly to his room through vacant pathways, unguarded. What was there to guard anyway . . . ?

Skin against skin, their bodies had taken on a third dimension: like a being born out of a miasma of eclipse and penumbra. Indeed the child bore a slender resemblance to his mother and curiously, his features had none the earthly grace of he himself. A niggling shadow of misgiving rose in his mind. Subsumed by passion he dwelt on it no longer. Effaced by obsession he neglected his own shadows, which weren't there, had he observed the infant objectively. *Was it then the Tibetan—?*

൭ ൏ ൚

His eyes fixed on the wilting stalks, Pu-Li thought that he had never been able to fathom her. The third being had consumed him bit after bit. Her sensuality—a mystique unknown in his country—and he had fallen into the snare. On his way back home, he had burned the astrological treatises in palm manuscripts, burned them in an impulse of rage and thwarted desire as for him Su-ko-ti's spirit carried all the beacons and understanding that a university never could supply.

. . . But did she really touch him?

In her presence, he could not read the nature signs any more than the sky. His eyes laden with an unknown emotion had dreamed up a drought-less world, thirty-three years back. Even then, her offering of love had transformed his memory to a mirror of inverted images—like yin in yang. Drunk in ardor, the stars had become a totem of plenitude. The softness of her breasts had blurred the vision of nature—sopping wet in a parched world; her compassion led him to pick on a blind course—blind to the celestial configurations as it really were then thirty-three years back. In the name of desire, he had forgotten his vocation even while he knew he would.

Li had mixed up tenderness and its shadows. His was a mirage of passion, but the Tibetan translator Chag Lotsawa, invoked magical *Bon* sutras to preside in the heart of Su-ko-ti.

He had thought of him as a friend . . .

Hidden in a corner of a pathway to a Vihara, he had slowed down his steps once and he had heard him speaking to Su-ko-ti of gSen-lha 'od-dkar—the god of white light: In nothingness, there emerged two radiant beams, one white while the other tenebrous. A rainbow then appeared, and from it there dawned motion and space, hardness, mutability, heat. Other times, he listened unbeknown and concealed in the veil of a hallway, the legend of gSen-rab, seated on a lotus— who ascended from the mystic land of Zhang-zhung, and whose alter ego was the Tathagata. Chag was humble enough to identify gSen with Laozi, the founder of Daoism. Indeed he was pleased that he met a comrade; thrilled as he learnt of Sa-Dag-lords of the soil who are propitiated before the seeds are sowed—the deities of the farm. *'Surely . . . he would tell his mother that.'*

Then, when he heard of the mythical kingdom of Shambala, which is located in China where the star of Vega would rule in golden times to come, his breast swelled with pride. He was taken in by the Tibetans exquisite world of ideas and allusions—his capacity to summon up wondrous aesthetic imagery. The Tibetan once confided to him, not without nostalgia, how the old gods were wearing a different attire and a stunning new pantheon was coming into being. They brooded in silence about how a shared cosmos evolved on different lines.

Slowly, over time, as he overheard the conversations between Su-ko-ti and Chag, he could identify the patterns. The translator of doxologies and the astrologer had struck up a rapport. He had thought of him as his confidant, even an accomplice. After all, knowledge was a weapon. Even sacred lore's must be used to sharpen the edge. Both of them were just agents of a higher power and control, that always and everywhere aspire for more. However, little by little, that bonhomie turned cool; Su-ko-ti's liking for Chag was more than mere admiration and awe. The Brahmins daughter had begun to treat Li patronizingly, or so he came to believe in spite of himself.

The starry-eyed Tibetan was trading icons of a kindred nature with the Indian girl. He, Pu-Li, of the poor farm of ever-cast skies, was becoming an onlooker of sensate games. Then, an old Chinese sage's adage became real:

個女子性質	A woman's nature
名男子的命運	A man's destiny
神不知 . . .	The gods know not!
我怎麼知道呢?	Who then am I . . . !?

'Funny hey!' he laughed loud and clear for the first time in his introspective journey.

He had kept his vexation screened. Slowly he invoked an ancient hubris that ran in his veins, for poor—though he may—he was still the child of illustrious ancestors whose legacy he must continue. Not to be looked down upon—never to be slighted again. Map after map, he revealed to the Tibetan Chag, the destiny of his nation. A wry smirk, an insuperable volition he began to exercise on the besotted pair.

No, she *never* really loved him. He knew that her birth Nakshatra was Anuradha and his was Moola. It was not to be. She was of the gods; he of titans. The handsome Tibetan was to return to his barren wind-swept country and he, drowned in his sense of defeat and shame, silently left for his misty village. There were no farewells, no parting whimper. He smuggled away with him a cargo of bitterness.

The farmer Pu turned his gaze against the sky of Laolin. He wasn't surprised that he could invoke his fading knowledge. It was lurking there all the while. From his memory, there issued forth the designs of heaven and earth once again.

Leisurely, with resolve, he steadied his arms. He had known his denouement and with a bamboo cane, he stood by his meager farm and drew his horoscope on the soil. A sudden thought flashed by— that what he was about to do, would correspond the same pattern to his country across the divide thousand years hence. Yet it was just a passing thought.

Mars and Saturn were in conjunction, the moon transits the Sieu of Pi, and the Saturn was unaspected in the house of Leo. Jupiter, in perihelion, had made its way in Capricorn.

Serpents weren't basking in the sunshine nor did the sparrows bathe in dust.

On the eastern horizon, there rose a magnificent rainbow.

Postscript:

A Daoist shrine still exists in Laolin. It had been built where the hutment of Pu-Li once stood. On his farm there grows genetically-engineered red kidney beans of incredible size and nutritional content. I was informed by the shrine-keeper that Li's memory is still revered. Some of his manuscripts are extant but I was denied access to the communal library where they are preserved. I couldn't help wondering that somehow the local chieftain got whiff of the fact that I was also an astrologer of some renown. Nevertheless, I never felt a dearth of human warmth during my brief residence-ship in Laolin.

I was surprised to hear from the shrine-keeper that the southern Ming dynasty had been replaced by the Hibiscus dynasty, which was even better. He could barely conceal his happiness. He said that the new dynasty had given him such a bountiful supply of necessities that he would last for another one hundred and fifty years. He was kind enough to show me the turquoise ring in the delectable ceramic box covered in the finest filigreed silk that the empress dowager Cixi had once presented him out of gratitude, for he had blessed her with eternal life one hundred and eight years back, when she came to pay homage to the Daoist shrine.

One night, as the smoke hung languorous, and clung on to my body, I felt the time has come for me to leave. Else, I reasoned, I would be sucked in by the elderly shrine-keepers enormous world of parables. Stupidly, I gazed at his drooping head and he began to *grow*. He loomed like a giant cloud; assumed different shapes ever so often, that I felt the cold drift of terror. He appeared to me like a master of the universe; I, a petty little atom. His ponderous demeanor seemed like a grand gesture of humility. As he talked about his heritage, his art, his culture; the timekeepers, who had preserved every moment since the dawn of time, like some precious jewel, my jaws hung low. I had just seen a few of the Sung dynasty prints of the great master painters and I couldn't help falling back to references and comparisons. At last, unable to hold any longer, I ran out crying—my heart, like a little bird—clinging on to a minutia of honor that a woman must have in order to get going. Since I realized that there was no comparison! Who would dare . . . ? Dynasty after dynasty, his country had created such a litany of grandeur—a quiver so full, so vast—*so simple in its basic complexity*—that tears streamed down my eyes. For a while, I felt blessed that my path should have led to Laolin. Indeed, for the first time, I became observant of a pilgrims consciousness, which I thought could never exist in me. I hobbled back to the shrine to bid a quick goodbye. It was necessary that I do so for courtesy's sake, even if it meant that I should disturb his slumber. Now, I recall, that he never slumbered. In fact, my instinct told me that *he knew* I would come back, even if that were for the sleeveless Pintuck that I had left behind in my dash. He bowed respectfully, offered me a cup of calming jasmine tea and as a token of friendship he gave me a carat-size lump of opium and a scrap of a timeworn scroll.

Today, I feel, I haven't left Laolin completely. A shadow of me will always stay there or perhaps I had become a shadow and had left behind my being, which was consumed by the shrine keeper who happened to be the namesake of the ancient astrologer.

Later, as I read the fading ink on the fragment of paper, I deciphered something that resembled floating images. The Chinese characters in the map I have presented here in English:

我的母親	My mother
我國農業	My farm
個標志	A sign
個要求	A calling
我的旅程	A journey
名女子	A woman
的愛心	Her love
道彩虹	A rainbow
攀夜盲症	Blindness
個打破夢	A broken dream
我離開	Departure
我國農業	My farm
我呼吁	My calling
個生命	A life
個枯死之夭夭	A withered blossom
我的命	My fate
個干旱	A drought

我已提這個圖表,_-我國印度朋友,這次我就不失敗,_會看到,再見:

I have asked this chart, you—my sweet Indian friend—this time, I will not fail, and you will see, good-bye.

Authoresses note: Here I present the chart in the current Indian astrological format from its traditional Chinese layout. It bears a faint resemblance to the 'dust bowl' prediction that happened in reality in the United States of America—year, 1939.

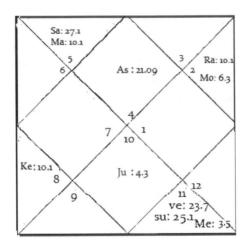

當我們應付在天國 . . . . 或地獄讓我們超越仇恨的干旱, 我們的心: when we meet in heaven or hell, let us go beyond the drought—hatred, and our hearts . . .

一個—大的球消防 . . . . 一個白光 . . . . 我可以看到: A huge ball fire . . . A white light I can see

我-應死於今天,我感到非常非常乾燥天氣非常乾燥, ... 的明星說: I, Li, should die from today, I am very, very dry—weather very dry, the stars said so . . .

I humbly admit that I could not make any sense out of the reading, as the exact time and year when it was composed, has flaked away over the millennia. Even this fragment, I had great difficulty in putting together.

*The Lu-shi-kang lake is now a military base where smart booted soldiers walk on water.
**Shambala is now a sprawling city of skyscrapers.
***It was raining, drizzly. Some curious questions arose in me as I travelled back on the Volvo bus that took me to the state-of-art airport from where I had to take off homeward.

Why was the Brahmins daughter so free with her care? Agreed, the dispensation at that time was such that the knowledge that had flown out of the university and burnt out of existence could only be brought back through some kind of trade. Could it be that the abbot in connivance with the Brahmin had made her a vehicle—that she should offer her body for scrap pieces of knowledge that remained only in the heart of foreign travelers? This nauseating assumption I dispensed promptly, for it bore a hole in my heart just to think about it. Was it then youthful indiscretions, which happen all times all ages?

A demure thought floated by. I smiled. Pu-Li's desire to possess Sukhavati could only grow over time. His reference to the Chinese adage about a woman's *character* and man's *destiny* . . . and so on, had an equivalent in Sanskrit *"Striyascharitram purushasya bhagyam devo na janaati kuto manushyaah"*, which kept me wondering for a while if a basic difference did exist in *the nature of things*!? Be as it may I put the M-player; Floyds 'Pigs on the wings' . . . *We'll zigzag our way through the bottom of pain . . . Occasionally glancing up through the rain . . .*

****In any case, the University of Nalanda and the characters, Rahula Shribhadra and Chag Lotsawa, are all fictional. No ghurid hordes ever invaded India in 1193.

****The land called Tibet never existed but it remains in the memory of the shrine-keeper as an exotic and beautiful emanation of the human imagination.

THE MIST

When I see my body, I see nothing. Well, not exactly nothing, that would be an exaggeration, but almost so. There's no substance. By having substance, I mean something that can truly be touched or its constituent parts can really be seen, or felt or perceived by the senses. That's what I lack and so I say I'm nothing.

I'm just a gossamer diffused sort of existence that wafts by vagrantly like wisps of remembrances.

At times, I'm being borne high, carried aloft by the winds and at times, I touch the ground. I move lightly, undulating like white sprays on the crest of a gentle wave. You all know that I'm the child of darkness and coolness and my body is made up of thin strands of vapor. You can see me clearly in mellow spring dawns but you can also watch me grow in the light of the moon and the stars.

The sun takes away the little existence that I have and so do the heat that comes in its fray; and when it rises high, I cannot bear the ache and I coalesce into dewdrops and then disappear.

The children of the earth get a little entranced by my presence and feel happy to be touched by me. They wish that I stay for a while more, for they want to partake of the languor that's my essence.

But there are other reasons for which they find me so inviting.

It maybe, that my tenuous mantle covers up the maddening array of things that surround them. To be obscured for a while perhaps makes them feel one with themselves. After all, too many objects and images can crowd out the little distance, they seek.

A little distance is what they wish for sometimes, but the drudgery of their lives affords them none. I cannot presume to understand their nature and I wonder if they themselves do. They are riddled with contradictions. They seek distance, even while they are touched. When they see me, they are perhaps reminded of the endless spaces back in time that made them feel unique and real and worthy. Little suzerains over vast terrains, but now they are all bunching up—cluttering up their lives and their thoughts, cramming the space that they dwell in.

It is not that they don't need touch. Indeed, touch is what makes them so. Touch is everything, but to be touched lightly; to listen to the voices as if they were coming from a distance, to see a face whose blemishes are obscured by a film of oblivion, is what they ask for sometimes. Else, they get mad!

. . . . Madness . . . as if it was a law.

This world is the stomping ground of a lunatic.

I do not know why I say so. It's just that it has made its haunt, every home and every habitat that I've come upon. Unbeknownst to them, it descends like a pall on their lives. Without exception, it makes every being its victim; much like the all-pervading reach of *Dukkha*. I cannot say whether Dukkha follows in the trail of madness or precedes it. It is so that madness is a state of mind and Dukkha is a state of being, but it could be otherwise. However, there is one thing of which I am sure of—that is there is no escape from their claws. How deep it digs is of course a matter of individual destiny.

Life is as much a struggle for survival as it is to be sane, and sanity is as elusive as living. It is a rare thing to be lucid as it is to be living; and it is the same thing to be lucid and to be living.

To be sane . . . to be happy . . . to be living! What wondrous ideas came by their minds? The drift of vanity I suppose . . .

When I hover high, I can see the earth, and it looks so splendid, so beautiful. But like beauty, it is so fragile. It is like the skin of a fig and yet it holds so much vanity. Perhaps, vanity is the mask that it wears to cover up the ugly face of sorrow, of madness, of existential anxiety.

Vanity is the buoy that saves them from drowning in a sea of nostalgia, from what is yet to come!

Am I then looking at the barren fields of nostalgia?

Nostalgia for a future that shall never blossom to Nirvana—that shall never see the becoming. The end of becoming.

Is it that hollow promise that makes them sad and drives them mad—the scorched gardens of Karma.

. . . I'm digressing again. Too much meandering can spoil the thin harvest of our blighted minds. It should be evident by now that I too partake of that ancient hubris that dwell in all things and which makes *us* think that we matter. But if we just confine ourselves to just seeing and cease to dwell on things, then everything would look brighter.

I can see the tree over there. I can see a forest. But that tree is different! It is too elaborate to be called a tree and too sedate to be called anything else. I see a shaft of light illumining the tree. Bright indeed! Wily moon! She has pierced through me again and has left a gaping wound. I can see her face but I can see the sodden earth too. I can hear the buzz of insects and other subliminal hum that flourishes with the night. Ascetic moths are floating by like blighted nymphs through my body, which has grown so vast tonight that my claws do not know where my mouth is. The bigger I grow, the wobblier I become. As it is, my body is not held by a center: There is No core, No skeleton, No tissue! It's just a vast abundant languor, lumbering through a maze of dreams, putting everything that it touches to sleep. And when I heed through the drift of their slumber I am astonished once more.

How their passions soar high like an eagle and they commit such perfidy as they dare not when they are awake. They violate their own laws and reign over forbidden territories. But then again, they would begin to lose altitude and the flurry of dreams settles slowly and they would think that they are being touched by grace; but it's me that they touch.

Today, I've stretched thus far. I do not know when my friend darkness shall leave me alone in the lurch. Whether I'll be a curtain of dew or a cloud or precipitate as snow. I do not know whether my enormous body will break up like a dream with the first stirrings of daylight or whether I'll be able to weather it for some time more, but alas, even as I speak, I see the fingers of light stroking my body. But today at least, I feel that it would be difficult for the sun to scatter me. I am looming like the bloated corpse of a white elephant and I'm anchored on nostalgia.

The tree too is anchored on nostalgia, I suppose, else why should I be drifting towards it! I see a man down there. He is emerging from beneath the tree. He stops in his tracks and turns his gaze at the eastern sky. He looks transfixed. *He is the Shramana*. The same Shramana, I've been watching for an eternity now. He always drags me into his thoughts. It is *he* who invoked me to rise again. It is my destiny to watch over everything and think of nothing and it is his, to think of what I think!

I don't begrudge him of course. Notwithstanding his mendicant mind, he has a certain delicacy of feelings that I often wonder could have been my own had I meditated on my nature. But my feelings are jaded and I'm besotted with darkness.

It's only today that I got a little carried away and in spite of me, vagrant anguished thoughts began to drift in. However, this moment, I feel so lucid that I find myself in perfect harmony. There is a magical levity in the deportment of things and I cannot explain why, but I suddenly feel different. There is no denying that that there is a touch of grace somewhere and I don't feel so heavy anymore. It just happened sometime back . . . this fading quarter of the night.

I see he is walking toward the river and it seems his feet aren't touching the ground. So light is his stride and so gentle a bearing that it's almost fragile, and yet is not so. I've never seen such an expression on his face. I've never seen such an expression on anybody. So beatific! So placid! Some kind of inward bliss is propelling him today. I can see his downcast eyes but there is a hint of irony in his smile. I wonder what he's thinking of—not about the world, of course!

There he comes to the gravelly banks of the river. Morning flowers are blooming one by one. So furtively do their petals unfold, as if their own virginal beauty embarrasses them! The wind is singing through the rushes and the river is so gay that I feel like returning to her bosom from whence I rose. But I've grown too vast and wandered too far.

There I can see the burning grounds, and the desultory smoke from the embers of the dying night shall become a part of my body. So too, shall be the preambular smoke of the sacrificial fires that shall burn throughout the day.

I can see a girl walking toward the tree from the village side. No, she isn't a girl, she's a young woman. It's strange that she comes at such an early hour. A mild breeze is blowing and she is trying to tie her hair into a bun, but it is tumbling down again. She needs more practice, I wonder. I cannot see her now that she is under the canopy, but there she's again, looking keenly at something.

His beautiful footprints have mystified her . . .

Wish I could carry on a little while longer. Wish I'm not dispelled so easily. But, I already feel the lightness and the inevitable waning has begun.

As if evanescence is the proof of my existence, generous world.

He stands facing the river. The early light is irradiating an aura around him and he appears like an angel. The night is receding beyond the western sky and the assorted song of the birds is heralding another cycle of wakefulness. One part of my extensive body is warping at the horizon together with the remnant of the night. It shall drag me along, like a veil across the radiant face of the new day. The young lady has begun to diffidently follow his trail that issue from under the tree and lead so far as the silver banks of the river.

The Shramana is still there standing as if in a trance and birds, bees and butterflies are trailing in from all sides presumably seeking nectar among the flowers. She probably couldn't see him yet. His track lies through lush vegetation and long grasses.

I am now so reduced, that just a mild breeze is able to bestir my repose. I'm beginning to get a sense of the nostalgia that the earth has for the future that it will not see. Oh mortality!

The girl has halted in her tracks and from behind an orchid tree, she's gazing at the luminous Shramana. That man is different. I know him since he was born, and I've followed him ever since. I know that I was the dream that he dreamt last night. '*Thou art I, O dreamer!*'

Two Sunbirds are flitting around him for quite some time now. One is of the midnight shade of blue and the other, its mate, is of the amber hue of the moon, now alights on his shoulders. 'Have they come to seek the nectar in the fragrant body of *Karuna* that is you, O Shramana?'

A few moments back you put all your papers in the incinerator! That's fine. That's OK . . . that's how it should be.

. . . Also the mask!? Very well . . . then

HELLO-OTTEH

BUMBLING PSYCHOPATH

[A scrap page from the diary]

CAVEAT 0: Wrap the cucumber tightly with a gauzy muslin cloth. Now with a shaving blade cut the cloth. If you manage to do it without even so as a scratch to the cucumber, then you've got the métier. I forgot to tell you that it should be a garden-fresh cucumber with a very fine skin and there should be just one fold of the muslin cloth.

I've been known to kill men by a process called *induced* hemorrhage. To induce hemorrhage needs no effort on my part. You don't need to castrate. You don't have to inject any venom, anti-coagulants or bio-chemical agents.

The basic assumption or first principle is simple enough. Let's not be too scientific. I enumerate.

Consider the equation: (it might be wrong for I'm out of math for a while, long while), nevertheless consider:

Man $x \rightarrow f^{-1}$ (m) $\{(. . . m$ in $M| f(m), . . . f($women $. . .) . . . . f$ (Memory $. . .) . . . . \infty\}$

Therefore—
Get to home.

a) Intuit the pattern of dreams and diseases by the pattern of the upholstery.

Like, for example, if the particular person has hemophilia, then most probably there won't be too many furniture's with jagged ends or he might not move around too much. He may even be wearing silk slippers. On the wall, there may be a print *La Mort de Marat* by Jacques David, but an unframed print. If he has Osteogenesis

Imperfecta or brittle bone disease then his furniture would be cushioned up soft and cozy and if, at all, he's got a print of senor Picassos' *Standing Nude And Seated Musketeer* then the concerned man's dreams are not his own.

b) If he has or has not any disease (which would be absurd), *notwithstanding*, take to empathy.

That is to say, become whatever he wishes to be at the moment. Listen to the intermittent series of psychic throbs that make him the bundle that you see. *That you are.* Talk about art, politics, history, women; ask about his ailments, his life. It doesn't matter who initiates the talking. *If he wishes silence, then be silent and compassionate. Compassion is the child of empathy after all.*

CAVEAT 1: This is important; that had he wished silence and demands of you to go away, then *you* lack empathy and it is you're failing. You have killed the killer in you. You're not up for the job.

You haven't understood the simple little equation. Well, it's a tad more than that . . .

Having said that, I add, that if you were making allowance for his silence and intuited it to be the interim-time, a gathering of his wits for the preliminaries, the overture or vice-versa; if you've sent a feeler and he reacts amenably to it (after a period of silence) then you're up for the job.

He has spewed out his reasons, his reckonings, his beliefs—the very squeeze and core of his being and existence, you stay calm and listen. You don't know something he's talking about, nod in commiseration. Do not in any way let him feel he's talking to himself. Add the right subjunctives at the right time. BE INTELLIGENT IN THE SENSE *THAT* HE *MUST BE WHAT REQUIRES OF* YOU. He wants to solve Fermat's last theorem? He's on the brink of cracking it. You never heard of Fermat. He wants to know if you know about the picture. You nod as though you know the artist himself. 'Who was his muse at that time friend,' he asks. You fumble.

CAVAET 2: Fool, if you have let him on this line or inadvertently pulled this plug, then you lack totality; you lack the sense the vision.

Your empathy is not sufficient. *You cannot arrogate to yourself all potential kingdoms.* You've failed the killer in you. Go to hell bloody.

But you've gone too far, held with your blood and toil—his attention, his rapture; so you skew the conversation in your favor—the things you know best. Wangle him discreetly tenderly to your path. THAT IS, TRANSMIT TO HIM *YOUR* NOTION OF EMPATHY, VERY *VERY* SUBTLY.

d) You have disconcerted him, you're towing him delicately back to the stream of words and your consciousness-moorings. Be very attentive while you are tweaking, turning, stretching him. Talk about Hahnemann, the Sutras, the Bodhicitta: anything that is alien to him.

It may not be alien to him. He may, after all, be the master of all trades.

Even then, he probably might allow. He might give you the benefit of the doubt. He might condescend. He's chuckling inside! Take to chiromancy. Read his right palm, the destiny he makes, unlike the left that is constitutional, given him by genes. Talk about the future. There both of you are in the dark, so you can be at relative ease.

Relative? Because his extrapolation of events from the past might just give him the edge: a better idea of the future; an empirical clairvoyant if you like. Don't underestimate.

Ease? 'Coz there could be anything in the minute progression of events—like the lightning outside that rattled the grid of the house—just now, and you predicted it a moment before and told him that it's about to happen. You have read the meteorological department's forecast of the day and your listening is keen. You thought he'll be impressed. He isn't.

Your insight of his past is stunningly accurate. 'Why?'—You ask. SEE BELOW, POINT 1).

He's not impressed!

j) Smile at him. An open smile as if you're the biggest fool in the world by his side.

e) Seek his blessings. Lend out your palms.

f) He starts to squeeze your palms (he won't if he's a hemophiliac or brittle-boned) that you perceive, is without love and delicacy and *if* he is averse to blessings, for he may just find it a high handed thing, then

k) Then YOU . . . YES YOU BLOODY OAF, *you bless him.*

CAVEAT 3: You perhaps have transmitted to him your conception of empathy but in the process you have lost a little bit of yours, which means you bungled again. This time it's too much for you? If it is so, then not doubting you are the fool—proceed. No way turning back.

i) Call the name of your own parents, your wife, your children, your relatives and start saddling them with wanton curses.

g) If you see him going for a gun, then say, 'Thank you, it's a pleasure . . . So long' . . .

You're malleable, so the bullet would whiz past you.

FLEE.

f) If he does not go for the gun, it's time to say goodbye. You wave at him three times with your right hand. You put your hat on and doff him. *If,* exactly, at the same time, while you were waving at him, he too had waved at you with his left hand —

❦

You must have left behind your cell-number along with your slippers, your pajamas, the underwear; The cell-number—a wrong number? You are wearing a hat and nude in the street you're spinning from one walk to the other. The telephone doesn't ring in a few days.

WAIT.

Most certain, you'll get a call back. But if you don't, then you've killed. At least assume you have. Be confident.

AFTER ALL, HE'S NOT YOUR NUMBER ONE AGENDA.

If you happen to have his number, don't call. Forget him.

Tring, Tring, Tring la-la . . . you're hoping, but it won't ring for you've assumed him dead.

❦

Call him someday from the telephone booth. Probably he's alive. If so, then assume a different voice. You *know* when he's at home so you can be sure. You know when he's alone.

Truly alone

1) YOU'VE DONE YOUR RESEARCH. You know his platelet count, his blood group. You know his age, his sexual proclivities; where he lives, in which country; his economic status, his educational attainments; his political leanings; whether he's in his skin or a gonner. His buying and selling habits. His police records.

You know since you're observant. For you have empathy and you relate to him.

If he says 'hello-hello', keep your quiet for a while. Then when you perceive he's about to hang up you say, 'Hello . . . .' You name him by his own name. A little diffident or a wild shriek.

❦

In the maddening crowd, someone has called his name. He can't recall. He cuts the line.

He falls asleep? You know he hasn't an aberrant gene that makes him an insomniac. That he is tired when he is. But too much tiredness makes one wakeful—and that you know.

Then in a deep dream of peace, he recalls you—your face, and blood begins to ooze.

And the bench at the park is wet with blood.

THE MYSTERY SHOPPER

MYSTERY SHOPPER WANTED
EARN NO LESS THAN $ 200.00
Need extra INCOME!
Become our [MYSTERY SHOPPER]:
Earn [NO LESS THAN $200.00] Per Venture:
It is Very Easy and Very Simple:
No Application fees:

Here's your chance to get paid for shopping and dining out!

Your job will be to evaluate and comment on customer service in a wide variety of shops, stores, restaurant and services in your area.

Mystery-shoppers are needed throughout the country!!

You'll be paid to shop and dine out, plus, you can also get free meals, free merchandise, free services, free Entertainment, free travel and more.

Great Pay. Great Fun Work. Flexible Schedules. No experience required. If you can shop—you are qualified!!!!

Let me explain to you what it entails.

What is a mystery-shopper?

A mystery-shopper is like being 007 at the mall. Mystery shoppers must complete their assignments and go un-detected. Mystery Shoppers receive assignments consisting of a variety of business types such as: restaurants, food chains, automobile dealerships, retail stores, and more.

Businesses benefit from the services of a mystery-shopper because they report their unbiased review from a customer standpoint. This enables the business to identify problems that could result in an unhappy customer and loss of sales. As you can see, mystery shoppers have a great responsibility and are paid accordingly. As a Mystery-Shopper you can:

- Earn up to $200 per assignment
- Have a flexible schedule and hours
- Pick and choose what assignments you want
- Bring your kids with you on assignments.
- Work part time or full time.
- Get free merchandise
- Get paid for dining out
- Stay at hotels for free
- Get paid for going to the movies
- And much more . . .

We will be sending you Travelers' cheque's or Money Orders for any of your assignments which you will encash at your financial institution and you use the money to carry out the assignment. You do not have to use any money from your pockets. So we will provide you the money for all your assignments.

What you need to do is to contact the email below
————@
The following information below will be needed:
Full Name:
Address (no Po Box):
City:
State:
Zip code:
Phone Number(s):
Age:
Occupation:
Email Address:

We look forward to working with you
Regards,
Dani Goodluck

❧

I'm hoomprey boogart, ey'hey. I'm hoomprey. No, I'm not wax.
I'm talkin' maan.

The fag is pasted. You mystery shopper too . . . I've something to say to you.

Hey, a moment of your time, please . . .

Not . . . me . . . my familieie . . . *your* familiele . . . the whole familiale . . . civilization man!

Hey, heeeyyy . . . Okay! Thanks tons.

"Old mother Hubbard went to her cupboard, to fetch her poor doggie a bone. When she bent over, Rover drove her.

He had a bone of his own."

Now I'm oomprey, so betta' listen. Proper tung. OKAY, TONG—tang—TONGUE. Yea . . . got it right this time. You really remind me of father, darling. So let me get my father's tongue. My father's story. But tongue . . . no tongue . . . I'm just so tired . . . I give you the story my father had penned before he became the product par excellence. You can find him in the aquarium

Yes, he was devout, Chriss and all! . . . No . . . but Raza Unida

Yeah I read it out . . . to you pops story . . . you won't understand his hand writing. So get ear:

*   *   *

My wife Monica was a mystery-shopper herself. Since I was married she was mystery shopping her body—in art colleges as a model, in literary establishments as muse and then here and there.

Jonny and Julie—my children, are mystery-shoppers too. They have stopped going to school for the teachers were in food courts, in theme parks, and in the cinema, mystery selling Johnny and Julie. That is to say, giving them free coupons to go to shops, where they swapped them to get their candies, ice-creams, jumping boots, manga videos etcetera.

At the end of the day Jonny and Julie brought home a sum 400$, while Monica was bringing in 600. I advised her not to go shopping her way as her means could be met by M-S. But she won't hear a word of it. Fine by me. How naïve!

I explained her that we are just a family of four and if we expend just a little energy, that will get us 800 quid a day—4500 a week a minimum, along with free lunches, travel vouchers, golf-club memberships . . . , but Monica was adamant, a pig-head, until finally students of the Fine Arts college began to bunk classes and she stood the pedestal, posing at the empty walls, to see her shadow and the literary circle which needed muse-wheedling began to lapse in their own orbit, until the circle came to be a point which was Monika.

Life is easier if we realize simple truths and stubborn refusal to logical propositions only complicates things.

Now it is evident, that for mystery-shoppers to take off, there must be mystery-sellers in the first place—coupons or not—for if you go with a money-coupon and there ain't any seller, then how can you give an unbiased feedback to the benevolent people who devised M-S, and who supply you the money in the first place. The money-coupon system had come alive and was as good and as well accepted as legal tender—good old jinni Monnie!

If you read the offer keenly then you'll realize that it's not just another old-style kind of market survey and you are not ordinary recruits. You're being paid beforehand by Dani Goodluck and you pick and choose your assignments.

Yes, there was a vague misgiving that this phenomenon is going to be just a short-term arrangement and the good-luck-charity would cease the day when say a thousand feedback of a product in question shall validate or vindicate it or render it rubbish. But as products come in all shades and varieties and tend to lose their color, flavor, climate and taste over time, the mystery-shoppers will survive. Yo!

In the wake of obsolescence, there arise new products, there is product diversification and in case of market-failure there is always the swashbuckling government with new and novel products . . . Oyo baby. Its bliss!

Now its years.

One such day, I wandered and I was beside myself with sweet and tender feelings and lest you think where I ought to arrive upon—it was the brothel.

Dig it man.

The pimp, who liked to call himself impresario, said you can mystery shop those on the lower tier. The upper tier was more enticing.

The products were so beautifully displayed; it took your breath away. So innovative: so mindful of design! Logically I could've actually got there but by spending my own money. This stalled my rush. I was reconciled to the fact that it was credit from Dani Goodluck and it shall always be credit in the form of money-coupons, even if I could see my wife's face pasted on the window—her upper body writhing, making serpentine strokes and grimacing in a howling sort of way. 'High hologram bar-coded products,' the pimp informed me quietly, and nodded gently. He offered me to swap the coupon for his own money but the very generosity of the offer carried a whiff of humiliation. Thus, out of decorum, I refused. He then said that I can always try the lower-tier, my feedback was highly esteemed, and a convivial whisper, 'In a few days' time the products up there shall crawl down and then you can M-S as much as you like to.'

I thanked him for this insight and was about to turn back, when a voice in my head said, 'You've come a long way comrade. *Why not shop.*'

Why not shop?

So, I entered the lower-tier of the hallowed institution. There were all sorts of experimentation going on. There was drinking and carousing and some real sport.

In an orient style cubicle, I met Julie. 'Shopping?' I asked. 'Time being I'm not,' she replied. 'But if you're looking for Jonnie you'll find him on the upper deck,' she added. Sometime lapsed, gabbing. I thought I'll go back home.

I lit a cigarette, as I leisurely walked back. The fiscal sentiment rose and I counted the yield estimate.

'Could be 200 or maybe . . . then 400. That's a max.'

I felt a pang in me; we missed out on the marginal 400 or 200.'

. . . No-NO Jonnie was up there. It's a proper brothel. For straight ones too. He must've spent . . . . It's a net zerooo. Sshucks!

I whittled it down with a puff of smoke.

* * *

Now that you've listened to my father's toungue—tung—tong . . . you scram. You, wuddup? Why're you standin' . . . you need this piece of paper. Take it, take it . . . Now truck-off man.

I'm hoomprey boogart,.ey'hey. HEY'E"'HEY MUCHO
    Hey mucho cardenalo, un momento . . . por favor . . .

CREATURES' ALL

Often I think of creatures. Of creatures who think of me.

Like the mantis resting on the tip of my penis. Like the hundred variegated moths all splendid and unique—fluttering on the bridge of my nose. Beautiful!

Like the flying roaches of enormous feelers, crawling about my nipples. The horse—who broke out of the polo ring with a dangling jockey—I ran with my kids to see the spectacle—and his formidable gallop became small trot when from a distance, he saw me.

Anna Karenina, my Russian Spitz, who took a blob of flesh off my calves and became rabid. They shot her, but not before a deep swathe of blood oozed from the flesh of my wrist—as the bullet, just a little deflected—hit her lungs.

I wonder of creatures who think about me.

The sunflower, that turned her gaze from the gloaming sun to catch my glimpse, as I was about to snip her; so too, the marigold drifting in Sal leaf, when the river delivered it to my neck.

The falcon, who dropped from the sky on my shoulder; the gold-winged butterflies that buzzed on her dying throbs.

The wilting grass grew the night of rains on my toenails. The black cobra, raising her hood—hover over my head—banishing away humanity, so to speak: her venom. The nightingale landing on her hood. Not the thorn.

Those who thought of me.

The rhino who gave her udders for me to get the thin flow of milk; I thought it must be thick.

Silly I am.

The downy plumage with vermillion eyes and sallow hue—head azure, marked with spots—saffron dye—legs a deep red-siren call of the flamingo. She coiled her neck around mine awhile, while her mates flew in such numbers as one might take them for a cloud. Pink clouds in the mush of rains.

Those past remembrances—like the Komodo whose skin I wear: the Minotaur, the centaur, the dinosaur.

Otters and cormorants in the yellowed lake Lu-shi-kang, who fed on my saliva—caught of fishes for me—only to be thrown back to the waters.

The grizzly, who licked my balls; finding the taste of silver, gave me warmth. The red salmons rushing home after the spawn, writhing on my belly.

Her halt.

Often, the grasshopper resting on the tip of the bulbous rhizomatous orchid—birds of paradise. The bird who should have been the serpent.

Epiphytes!

A silent mist fall on me.

The green frog, yellowed in the bile of a horse, the green viper, dissolving in the four-fold stomach of the centaur. The redheaded bird, so far away, fawning, like wonder-peckers—its beak, like the red-head reed snake.

It's a bloody Mandala.
Humankind.
 As if I were human.

Two Sentinels

This December day is overcast. The stadium, all but empty. It's a bleak day for them. If they catch a fever, of course they can't write the term.

Not so Kalupal and Jaypal and the man.

He laid the crutch down, lit a cigarette and reclined under the orchid tree. Abundant with heart-shape leaves, the tree shot sprays of pinkish-white blossoms. If from a distance you see an orchid tree, they're much like cherry blossom. Perspective!? Not pretty maids in a row. Just one.

He picked up the zizzz' trickle and knew Kalupal had sneaked in from behind. Kalu leaves her ludicrous trail, lest she loses her way and she must perform her ritual ablution.

❦

I silently moved a close, hid behind the nettle bush and watched. Ever since I was eleven, I had admired him. There beneath the boughs, a crutch, a smoke and thou: *beside me is singin' in the wilderness—wilderness is paradise enow . . .*

He's like the elder brother we call here 'Dada,'—I *ne'er* had.

There is dance, there is energy, his split passes; sudden bursts of speed and equal decelerations that leave the defense gasping for breath. One of a kind. Midfielder!

Madam Kalupal lapped the scar in his nape. Ummm. She's got beautiful eyes, full of *pathos* and between puffs of smoke, Dada turned to kiss her behind her ears, as and when she pleased.

He observes the ball and not the man, close in unsuspectingly and with an elbow swivel, the referee can't cry foul, he flicks over dawdling in to measure the team.

I was once witness to his squeeze of her tits. Dare I not tell how Kalupal reacted, for if Dada happenchance comes to know that I'm on the look, then ba-god I'm nettle.

Kalu is lissome: trim waist, gleaming white teeth and the way she dominated Dada, was marvel. She leaped—stood astride, snuggled, cocked her ears with Dada under her arch and let out an inward snarl. There she was, laughing—Dada's pet 'determinist.' One man's!

He lessens his body as if midair, bows low his own goalkeeper and then swivels languid to chip the ball—the striker not off-side. That striker *is* offside—*his*? Nope, not his concern . . . uuuups!

Jaypal came loping down. Fifty yards he slips to swish 'ome nother' twenty. Kalu's eyes brighten up. Caked with mud and smelly beyond redemption he towed toward her. He had the special affinity for the earth. Nothing was repulsive fo'im. He would make a meal of dead ravens, or a limp stork; chew on leaves if the situation so deems: eat earth, clumps of grass.

He slots home the ball, fobs with it and lets it wait on the goal line—a hemisphere there and here. Ambles back.

'Agonizingly close . . . tisss!' as the commentator sighs.

Ah, but my computation, people say
I've squeezed the years to human compass, eh!

I hold a thing against Dada. Forgive.

I've ne'er seen him bring anything for Kalu and Jaypal, anything nice. This isn't to say, I think of him as miserly or abstemious. Haps' fallen into disrepair. Out of job. Something.

Absent.

O yes, he doth indeed supply Jaypal with snuffed ends of cigarettes and patronizes Kalu with Perfetti chewing gums!

'Everything's Matter—no-matter,' was air 'round Jaypal. Sometime strident, sometime cowed, depending on flesh or grass—he was the tramps 'Materialist.'

No matter, he played well. His very presence was jolt. Better player than him was 'pudd' by his leaden. A left-legged, he had more than foresight. A mother-fucking expletive uttered so quiet, graciously; Father-fuck rare, when his flagging ten betrayed.

⟡

It's overcast. Gray sky, I ain't sleep all day so I heed-head droop—droop. I have to. Time and time, I rub my eyes to get rid of the drowse. For I know and I know that ev'n in languor he's constant, awake, alert.

Midfielder's instinct?

It might even be so that he'd heard the quiet rustle behind the nettle but just pretending to be oblivious of the noise. Sticky hoe!

I clobbered on even when they made love with him; Jaypal nibbling at the nylon track pants. Kalu licking his face—slurping and sniffin' his groin—now on top, now there—the reclined man mostly unmoved, feeding them with Perfetti's and Navy-cuts. Grand!

Black 'o' white, the two sentinels gamboled, chased in rings across him,— sniffing arses', mounting, thrusting—bitin', hidin' . . . Ev'r to return. I'm bluey, weary, wearing his jersey. It's a fade. After the championships cup he'd given it to me. I was hollering for attention.

⟡

Ought I be party to the nonsense that's rooming in round him. Well enough! One of us must tarry, so I do.

The circuit of overarching boughs presents to me a scene of great magnificence. Jaypal, I see, is chewing on and on, all the li'l orchid petals strewn around the canopy, spitting out the stamens. Why Mr. Materialist? *Some choice.* He's just devoured twenty filter-ends, saliva dribbling and is still famished. He's five cubits in stature yet can't reach for the flowers which hasn't fallen own accord. Somethin' like 141 blooms, I've counted so far . . .

Kalu's gleaming white incisors and molars, like stars in a row of blue-red fangs. Thanks to the Perfetti's. She's content. From time to time, when she's done with the gums, she lifts her left *left* hind leg right on top of Dada's shaggy hair. Unlike Jaypal's wonder-less mind, Kalu is sweet to answer every sigh and call to nature.

It must be drizzling now. I feel wet but somewhere twenty yards from this shrubbery, under the tree, Dada's dry. There, the weather must be gential, for the fickle wind brings to touch the warm squall.

In the course of a few years, if Jaypal permits, then young daughters would grow around the mother tree. And, in that enclosure—shadowed and protected by the ramparts of stems— shepherds and pilgrims would find shelter by the rain and the storm, if elder brother dispenses his charity.
. . . So would the warmth in chill nights.

The time being, the threesome Mr Mrs JaypalKalupala and the big-time star are territorial, cozy and opposed fierce to intrusion.

Maybe, I don't give off pheromones deep enough like him.
Thank god for that. I won't like mongrels to lick open wounds. NO WAY baeybeee!

For now, I'm wide awake. Alert. A thorn did it.

Dada has slipped into a reverie and all the blooms are fallin'

KUMBHAMELA-HARIDWAR

[These are the reflections of a heathen. We pay tribute to our unknown heretic wives who we burned.]

We were men and we haven't ceased to walk. We were men burnt in the sun; our tresses browned and matted. Men made of clay with long flowing beards. Some of us fell by the wayside and the strong among us strapped them over, over our shoulders and moved.

A disproportionate number crawled, pierced themselves, got stuck in the melting tar or in flayed ribbons of tyre-rubber. Our haunches ached, knotted were our spine; by night we gutted up a few scattered bivouacs, and under the asterism of *Abhijita* we kindle the fire, cook a broth of stale cucumber and rice water. We stole cattle-bran and small mustard oil to flavor. The wise: the ventriloquists mow, made milk from unsuspecting cows.

An hour or a two of deep sleep and as pre-dawn light temper the oval sky, we set forth. At those points of departure, we put our foreheads together. We invoked the wind of karma to dispel the manifold multiplication of boils around the Ajna-Chakra and made a circle widening with each three-mile, milestone. And there, we summon our mother, long since that we have met her—to give us warmth, to guard us, to brush away the chill set of the fading night.

We pray. Utter the secret.

❦

We were unwashed and naked. Not a single band of unstitched cloth: not a shred. And, if in our sight there was to be a sick child, a dumb, broken woman, a eunuch, a misanthrope, we relent. Whatever we had we lay in our palms; we reached out and gave away the broth that remains in fullness—even the tridents, the crumb's, our beards, little fingers, chopped thumbs. In our recollect, none of us withheld; for we listened to the murmurs in our quivering breasts and we came to the conclusion that we must offer to them whatever little we possessed, not as penitents or pilgrims (that distinction was lost on us), not to expiate or to attain karmic-merit—but to silence the long remorse that afflicted us like a lacerating tissue in our memory.

In benign moments: in sweet enchanted spells, we meditated on the question of the Being: assorted, constituted—of the vagrant flow of energy and stillness, which of themselves, do not have form and therefore can neither be grasped by the senses or the intellect! Yet we tarried in the fortuitous combination of Names and Forms; ran after her, and she chased us: held us with her vice-like grip.

☙ ⸬ ❧

ORPHANS: Coz' we were as orphans; we often thought of what orphans may feel; what they ought to know. But, those were passing sentiments like anything passing. We never pondered over them than we deemed necessary. We saw the stoop, the knot in their spine.

A bewildering array moved forward as though there was nothing to turn back to. The ventriloquists. So be. It was impressive. That is not to say there were no link; indeed there was—for those who proceeded forward knew intimately and exactly those snaking backward—but with the difference that we never failed to notice that, both likewise, being givers and orphans and unhinged, those who proceeded forward were begging for alms.

To carry on was creed.

Thus our trail led to the city made famous by the seers, Haridwar! It is, they say, the gateway to heaven: the *fierce* paradise. Heavy was the root of our life, yet, and so entranced was the spirit of the valley that lay beyond, it seemed effortful to carry on further.

We lost trace of the cohort who hobbled behind and those ahead who trudged unceasingly in battle-speed. The schism vast. Not to say the child, the woman, the old man, the misanthrope. *Yes*, we remembered them; a touch of dignity lay somewhere; between us, and the gossamer. Lao says: '*Honor is a contagion as deep as fear*'— and the river was so vast, so utterly vast, it was flowing everywhere.

103

Perhaps, in a context different, we neither had honor nor fear, nor fear, nor contagion.

We say that for among us were the afflicted: those still suffering from small-pox; leper men, the syphilitic, the immunodeficient; our kin—the blood-hounds of Manu who in primal days knew the *converge*; for it is *not* nectar that the gods brew for the mortals. They brew it for reflection, for orgy-sake, and they won't spread a drop for men, to crawl around for the infinity of time.

. . . And the dumb, broken woman, heavy and pregnant, floated in the nectar.

Without her fullness, the valley ran dry.

A presentiment: the sick child could have been hers; the old man who got stuck in the tar, melting cauldron of her way: the misanthrope, the sage.

Water-bearer quenched the sun; made its way. Mars in Leo . . . whistling; and battles rage yet again . . .

❦

It was her eyes that held *us*. Rapturous. It was her lashes in particular: dewed shards, long and well-deep, and beneath the heavened lids—the membrane, the tissue, the iris, the corona—reflected like spars of radiant circles.

It appeared to us that there was no confession left in her eyes. That is to say, her eyes had the demiurge-like appearance of a coiling serpent.

An emerald halo lit; could've lit up the sky but the grotesque time-clock stood erect to obscure that wholeness of vision. Long shadows wove out of the women's changing room—dappled sunlight—they looked like so many moths with charred wings, lightly borne up by the mist issuing from the river by the holiest dip *Hari-ki-pauri*—where it is said, Vishnu set his feet on earth, and so, and yet so distant, dotted, we barely could imagine.

They splashed like silver sprays in eventide and then they too dispersed. Forgot. Little children fished out the coins (offered the river by the devotee's) with amazing dexterity and of course, their refracted vision helped.

Faith force *in us*!

We were in a deep triangle: the time-clock, the changing-room and where we gathered round to gaze at the proliferate of eyes. The minute hand and the hour, hung like a forked clit. The dichotomy was lost on us and we echoed the medieval: That Spencerian space of evolution like as in biology, applies in every science and genera; that it could explain not only specie and taxa but the planets and stars; social, political, economic history and aesthetic conceptions, and that theory alone can explain the evolution of matter and mind; from the savage to the distant recede of the stars and the spots. And so we thought, weighed, slept over it; rejected.

Mercury was in deep combust—a mirror led another. Hither thither we went in revolutions. Dervish-like.

As the clock struck even hands, the silhouette of a woman's body, sharply outlined, struck out own accord, out of the changing room, like a detached metaphor; gulped the cohort in a swipe of her tongue.

We jutted out in unison and because our male-members were equally proportionate to some given ratio of the spirit, not an ink of envy came pass us. Those out of herb, saw the milky in darkish gyrate of the hips.

༚ ༖ ༙

The long, flowing beard was now gray. Time had taught us to respect. So, we beat out our fists like hammer on anvil. But we dissolved as we realized that the water was thick like plasma.

༚ ༖ ༙

The hiccup—one of us: incessant jarring on the nerve. We advised him to hold breath. We did Reiki. We knocked at his solar plexus.

He throbbed.

After a while, began to stream.

The trickle flowed and all we could hear (ceteris paribus) was the call of return.

———◆———

THE FRINGE-RISHIKESH

They are not the nomads that the word suggest. To be sure, they had pitched their camp at the outliers of Rishikesh, and had slowly made ingress into the holy locales in amorphous waves—Haridwar, Pushkar, and Rishikesh—got their caste certificates issued by the government. Their faces had assumed the settled expression of agglomerates' people and no more were they the exiles they once were.

One thing though, their eyes (especially of the women and the children) if we are to go by physiognomy, were deep, dark, restive, buzzing-bee like, betraying just that small little corpuscle of evolutionary forging of hundreds of years of desecration. When seduction and appeal fuse and can carry home an extra change, then all societal sanctions fall apart like a house of sand and yet if you observe close enough, some latent madness flicker, like guttering candles.

For how long they've come to roost there was no telling, no specific data. It might just be that they were not the nomads or *Banjara's* in the first place. They could be of the *Bhangi* caste (cleaners, sweepers, scavengers) but they liked to introduce themselves as Banjaras, for that coin, perhaps, sanskritised them, a higher rung in the caste-tableaux of the government of India—their economic entitlements being the same. Then again, being on the fringe, the Banjaras had lesser political rights than the Bhangis, who were the more constituted with a parliamentary pedigree of not so recent vintage, for the founding father of the Constitution of India was the enlightened outcast. The god of shit and corpse.

When indifferently our hero Amaru had kissed full on the lips a scavenger beauty, a fatwa was declared. But that was long time, morning—July 1987, when he was fourteen and had just recovered from amoebic dysentery. The fatwa was revoked, when at the rectal end of a homespun revolver he snapped his sacred thread. With a memory and a theory like that on his mind, Amaru bought a beautifully embroidered second-hand sweater (his only purchase of some value in Rishikesh) for his sister. He then threw the polythene bag where the sweater was ensconced, saw it heave and shoot up and down and straight like a cuttlefish before it landed right at the center of the river as it gashed past. He wore the sweater and thought of it fantastic fit . . . 'If only it hadn't been embroidered . . . !' . . . And then drifting a long way, as if bohemian, he came upon the designated spot.

'That's a woman's wear!,' she squealed and split her sides laughing, while a child with her bottom upturned dug her head into the sand. It was the riverbanks and a jut in the crag of the guarding granite outcrops gave them shade.

'Eh daughter of a swine, if I ever see the child eating sand again, I'll chop your breasts and give it to the dogs . . . . Okaaaey'— Amaru growled in a peculiar Hindustani.

'Sit, sit by me. Will you please . . . here . . . here,' she spread a red cloth on the sands and smoothened it. '. . . All the time he's shouting his heads off,' she whispered to herself, audibly.

'She's stinking like turd . . . now will you or you . . .'

As his menace didn't cut, Amaru held the baby by the waist and flicked it over, and before she could break into cry he hunched, blew on her face a cheek-full of air and made a hissing cobra-like sound. The baby gazed at him wide-eyed and incredulous and let out a tiny silver hand sprayed with mica and brushed his nose and then like an automaton turned over bottoms up and head in the sand.

To make a stir about her would argue him to be a fool and also for other reasons Amaru shifted his haunches so as to position himself looking at the rock face instead of the river and the child.

A blithe wind was blowing and the Banjarin touched his shoulders lightly and ruffled his hair. All the chakras seemed to spring out of his body but he composed himself.

'Don't drag me into the bargain, alright? Now if I ever see you groveling, you know what I got to do?'

She answered back, 'Everybody tells me she couldn't be yours, she couldn't be yours . . . she couldn't be Laku's. There's not even the faintest resemblance . . . But it's when they tell she couldn't be yours . . . Why . . . Doesn't she have my lips, my forehead, my brows, my nose . . .'

'O yes perfectly . . . She'll grow up to be a slut never mind. Are you still doing it or not . . . stuffing up your arse . . . ,' snapped Amaru

'There you go again . . . now come, rest in my lap. The sweater looks good.'

'It's for sister.'

'It's a beautiful flower and leaf design.'

'It's for my sister.'

'Ah, how's she?'

'Usual . . . where's Laku?'

'He's usual in the hole . . . Out . . . You care a rap . . . Rest now.'

A certain time elapsed. He was in a *haveli*, a big deserted mansion with blind-alleys and 'not so blind' alleys and gaping holes for windows and doors; just the decaying wooden framework. Testimony of former age? It was his school perhaps, but he felt queasy. It was not. Such a school couldn't hold Mr. Bloud.

'. . . Are you still telling the story of the exorcist in graphic detail after your algebra lesson, Sir? Are you still enamored with me for I could draw the world map exactly? 'Charles Farrow's' world, with your honey-dew Gold flake cigarette smoke, twining into our pickled nerves. And, dear Mr. McNamara, I've heard you've shifted to Canada—I your reincarnate Scot muse, your best essayist, good in sports . . . excellent defender . . . The slim blue report card.'

. . . There is a catch. He tiptoed to the bracken, fallen green door; and right he was. There was no enclosed bracket, no railing, no veranda—just square holes at the level with the façade where sunlight billowed in, in maudlin patches. He held on to the wet wood and saw below, underneath, a green pool, a stream that had dried up, with hard crusted mud-banks; some pale-faced boulders on the other side. As he fell, he wasn't sure whether he'd drop onto the other side or in the middle of the pool.

Small chance.

A prank is being played out; many an innocent children have been murdered that way. But why? By whom? The decrepit building is like Hawamahal, a conduit of coolness in a hot dry land. No, it is not Rajasthan. It is the church of Saint James, Calcutta. Ecclesia et Patria . . . Our land comes next, our Patria, This land of Ind where

God has cast Our lot that we with service true May bring to her some treasures new.

To swell the glories of the past;
Ecclesia et Patria.
Hail, Alma Mater, hail, all hail; all bloody hail hail hail
Hail hail hail BLOODY
Hail hail hail
Hail Phila hail Phila
Hail hail hail

Philomena, you are different. On the first day of Christmas my true love came to me . . . nigh . . . na na na na . . . naii na na na na. I'm the hero, the best athlete . . . the Para's you read out to all Mr. McNamara . . . nil to nil . . .

When he woke up, he saw two huge black crescent pools gazing at him and half dozing and felt to touch on his chin the tender, muffled, warm, fetid breath—a cyclical chorus, muttering a garbled lullaby; bony fingers, drawing furrows on his shaggy head.

Very slowly, he held her hands up lightly and slipped out to see the sun in the exact position behind the transmission tower, where he had seen it last.

☞ ⟐ ☜

The river slows down this time of the afternoon and Xerxes-like Amaru felt the need—the great desire to lash it, to fetter it, to brand it with red-hot iron.

He took out his notebook and his ballpoint pen from the jean-green bag and scribbled . . .

2) That obsidian eye
    My hollow well
    Let then you peer again?

3) Go then near the sea
       An obscenity
       There is a cemetery hey

I'll cut a rose for you
This select day
    On this departed quay
    You may drop a silent mist
    I'll palm it off to great immensity

Why have I fallen to violence?

5) I was frail: You let me be
    And I had a wish for frailty
      I touch your hands
      A skein of geese
      Flowing nimbly as in a V
  Then shall I wait
    Eternity

4) I feel the urge to contemplate
    To rue: to trace the lines of your fate
    One drachma for a change
    And if it weren't enough for champagne
    You asked for that lonely kiss
  And what I offered and you won't know
    An inlet

So why have I fallen to violence

6) The tenor the musik the jewel the solace

    Dance bar swirling
Butterfly eye
    And on the steps
    Rose the prana
    Holding on to the balustrade.
Sibylline wind of blummer sleep
And you in me the silent steps
    And the telephone

So why have I fallen to violence

Add to 4)

> You know the truth: you and me (?)
> Nor shall we ever be

1) What happened to your lucid stripe?
       Your simple hand your warm smile
            Your kiss I took to paradise

Why have I fallen to violence

'Why, I wrote it at twelve?' He pondered on it for a while and scratched it out in a diagonal ray. It rang a false coin. He was losing his feel for language, meter, space. 'A sixth grader could write it . . . Man.'

The transmission tower was towering over the hills. Amaru became self-conscious. 'Why do I hanker after things foreign? Isn't this Banjarin enough . . . There are bridges to be burned, there are bridges to be crossed . . .'

'. . . Ey sleep na,' she spoke in her trance.

'. . . You sleep, I'm done.'

She stretched out one arm and pillowing it, her breath grew heavy. He swiped her emaciated body and it descended on him that even her parchment is beautiful.

'*Matisse*!' cried Amaru within.

Slowly he crossed the bank, climbed up the hewn-stair rock-face and entered the street. Half a mile away, he telephoned Ajay, his medical representative friend.

'Can't get any! How many times do I say?'

'I'll pay you extra.'

'Listen, this things going to end. The American NGO has stopped their direct supply of Efavirenz 600 and. Tenofovir. I've told you that they've come to know that we sell for a price. I'd rather that you contact them personally. I can give you the number . . . Why don't you take her to the mission.'

'She won't go . . . even Philomena couldn't persuade her. At least send me that . . . that er . . . It's very advanced tuberculosis.'

'Oh, that, I'll send—Rifampin. It's a new drug and it gets along good with HV drugs, but you have to pay forehand . . . you know I'm being monitored. Any day I can lose my job.'

'Fuck you won't . . . . OK . . . then when?'

'Next week . . .'

'Next week . . . when?'

'Say, by Wen'sday.'

'I'll tinkle Tuesday morning . . . bye—Thanks.'

Amaru went over to the grocer on the other side, got a few Cadburys' bar, a bottle of Horlicks and then on to the money-changer to change four Euros, fifty dollars—the remaining foreign currency and on the way back he met sister Philomena of the Syro-Malabar Catholic Church—the lone church of Rishikesh ; its stucco yellow cornice chipping off. Rather he banged into her unintentionally and sprayed all the homework notebooks in domino.

'Sorry Philo, sorry,' and he gathered them up in a foot-high stack and assuming the penitents mien he wished her, 'Good afternoon sis, how're you're titties?'

'They're fine. Thank you. How are you doing?'

'Very fine. Thank you.'

'What lesson?'

'Finished the endocrine system and begun with reproductive . . . thank god it didn't rain today.'

'You're a big show-off Philo . . . You could use a carry bag. How's father Manuel—the black. Is he again in Kansas, masturbating?'

'No darling, he's getting married to sister Bacilli.'

'Jezebbacilli!'

'You know Amaru, you're cross-eyed myopic.'

'O sister, I lack the depth of vision. I need to be close to find my binocular sight.'

'You seem to know biology better than my kids,' Philomena said; her gaze upturned and ethereal.

'No Philo I'm a poet,' said Amaru and then his voice was very soft, a whimper, '*Out of the window perilously spread . . . at night her bed . . . on alter are piled, stockings, slippers, camisoles and stays . . .*'

'Mischievous child 'o' mine. You remember just that part from *Prufork*.'

A high, cold wind spread out her veil and she repeated, 'Naughty child . . . it's thawing up there. Can you listen to the turbulent gush?'

'My tympanic membrane . . .'

Amaru offered her a Cadbury bar.

'Thank you . . . Bless lord . . . listen keen.'

❧ ⁂ ☙

Sprightly, intoxicated by the coolness of the sudden thaw—within, sister Philomena rumbling, he entered the OM jewel shop. Yes, he had to deposit his purchase to the sentry who twirled his oiled mustache and winked at him. 'Bomm Bhole.' Amaru gave him a Cadbury before he entered. The lighting was a subdued sodium-vapor lamp with hidden neon-tubules that gave OM the trans-luminescent green-blue-gold and the jewels, the gemstones as sharp as in the tower of London, the true image of his true desire, lit up Amaru's heart. Nothing else matters, Bruce-Lee, enter the dragon, and the angled, octave mirrors highlighted his hundred-fold image. He saw his reflections. '. . . Bloody barber shop . . . . Ahhh my beauty gone . . . . time to take ANTI-Oxidants.'

A single solitaire gazed at him.

'Dum . . . Mr. Moissanite, your refractive index is more than Mr. Diamond's but on the Moh's scale you're 0.8 beneath. I'm falling in love wid'u . . .'

And Mr Moissanite replied, 'Oh yes, all matter for you is the Moh's scale, shame . . . . I'm twenty six-thousand rupees—two carats . . . Won't you?'

'You're the product of a fallen meteorite M . . . Sheer chance.'

And M hushed, 'I love you.'

'Et tu . . .'

M appealed, '. . . And how should I begin; to spit out the butt-end of my days and ways. . . . And how should I presume?'

'Why so thundercunt Eliot!' inquired Amaru.

'Coz they're making pure allotropes, indistinguishable from real natural diamonds from . . . from . . . Human hair. They calling it cultured diamonds.'

'Remind one of a Maupassant short story.'

'But I'm the handsomest.'

'Handsomest! Well well . . . errr . . . yes you caught my attention first. Yet, is that the reason, thundercunt!'

And M said, 'Look around you.' So, Amaru looked around his reflections and saw him so handsome this time—HIS PRIME . . . LO—and was he not a little struck, for a few minutes back he was slunk, stricken, dark. And now he was shining. Wow!

'Where's your hat?' queried Mr. M.

'It's with sister Philomena. Her head, her eyes, her face, deep within . . . ,' Amaru smiled. 'Its silk lining is wet . . .'

'Bloody narcissist,' snarled M. 'Bear in mind you're gettin' old. The golden, smooth, reflections are my own image.'

'You too . . . Hmmm . . . you're silicon carbide and not crystal carbon.'

'I've greater refractive index . . . Mind you' M snapped.

'Eh mon,' smiled Amaru. 'I'll dong on your head with a diamond hammer and check your Moh's. Can you take me to the gong hills . . . ?'

'You seem very cultured . . .' M threw a gambit. 'Out of Africa, African Safari or the English patient?'

'English patient.'

'Comprador Class . . . ,' spewed M.

'Not a comprador but class . . . soreee,' Amaru humbly answered. 'And . . . O . . . yes . . . I'll give you to the woman stranded on the bridge . . .'

M whispered softly, '. . . and what shall you give to the woman stranded at the banks and the sand child . . . ?'

Slow on the uptake as he was, Amaru twirled the mustache of the burly sentry, gave him a piece of amethyst brought for a price of zero, tried singing Joe Cocker-style, his arms levitating, flailing nervily.

> *Come down off your throne*
> *And leave your body alone*
> *Somebody must change*
> *You are the reason*
> *I've been waiting so long . . . Somebody holds the key*

. . . And down the slippery granite steps—the moss-agate boulder, darkening with teeming thaw—he could see, but he saw no bottom upturned.

No sand child.

. . . Only a woman lying, with the waters lapping her shin.

———————•———————

Notes & References

OF LOVE AND TRUTH:

1. Naguib Mahfouz, *Sugar Street, Cairo trilogy III*. Translated by William Maynard Hutchins and Angele Botros Samaan (Black swan publishers 1994), 11, Chapter 1.
2. Naguib Mahfouz, *Palace of desire; The Cairo trilogy II*. Translated by William Maynard Hutchins, Lorne M. Kenny, Olive E. Kenny (Black swan publishers1994), 358, chapter 35, second-last para, 3rd and 4th line
3. Ibid, 358, last para
4. *Palace of desire*, 18, Chapter 2, second para, 1st, 2nd and 3rd line

TARA:

5 & 6. The author is grateful to Dr. Onkar Prasad who has translated so beautifully, the song's 'five mango leaves' and 'the night dew of the sky' into English, from their original in *Santhali*. It's a ccosmogonical view of a people in India (the Santali's) whose emanations are the songs. Interested readers can refer to this web-site: http://ignca.nic.in/ps_01014.html: Primal Elements in the Santhal Musical Texts by Dr. Onkar Prasad.

Dani Darius spent his childhood in Calcutta and subsequently moved to Delhi. There, for a short while he taught comparative economic development in a campus college. His interests range from heterodox Indian thought and Tibetan Art to Hats and Perfumes. He works as a soccer coach in Noida.